WAR AND PEACE
BOOK ONE : 1805

By Leo Tolstoy

War and Peace Book 1
by Leo Tolstoy

Copyright © 2022

All Rights reserved.
No part of this publication may be reproduced, stored in a retrieval system, or transmitted in any form or by any means, electronic, mechanical, photocopying or Otherwise, without the written permission of the publisher.

The author/editor asserts the moral right to be identified as the author/editor of this work.

ISBN: 978-93-94973-10-7

Published by
DOUBLE 9 BOOKS
2/13-B, Ansari Road
Daryaganj, New Delhi - 110002
info@double9books.com
www.double9books.com
Tel. 011-40042856

This book is under public domain

Printed in India.

About the Author

Leo Tolstoy was a Russian creator known for his books War and Peace which is viewed as the best book of pragmatist fiction. Tolstoy is additionally viewed as world's best author by quite a few people. Additionally an ethical scholar and a social reformer, Tolstoy had extreme moralistic points of view. In later life, he turned into an intense Christian rebel and anarcho-conservative.

Leo Tolstoy Born in Yasnaya Polyana on September 9, 1828, He had a place with a notable honorable Russian family. He was the fourth among five offspring of Count Nikolai Ilyich Tolstoy and Countess Mariya Tolstaya, both of whom kicked the bucket passing on their youngsters to be raised by family members.

In 1844, Tolstoy was acknowledged into Kazan University. Incapable to graduate past the subsequent year, Tolstoy got back to Yasnava Polyana and afterward invested energy going among Moscow and St. Petersburg. With some functioning information on a few dialects, he turned into a multilingual. Yet again the recently observed youth pulled in Tolstoy towards drinking, visiting massage parlors and most betting which left him in weighty obligation and anguish however Tolstoy before long acknowledged he was carrying on with a brutish life and endeavored college tests with the expectation that he would acquire a situation with the public authority, yet finished yet up in Caucuses serving in the military continuing in the strides of his senior sibling.

In Year 1862, Leo Tolstoy wedded Sophia Andreevna Behrs, generally called Sonya, who was 16 years more youthful than him. The couple had thirteen youngsters, of which, five passed on at an early age. Sonya went about as Tolstoy's secretary, editor and monetary chief while he made two out of his most prominent works. Their initial wedded life was loaded up with happiness.

He started composing his show-stopper, War and Peace in 1862. The six volumes of the work were distributed somewhere in the range of 1863 and 1869. With 580 characters got from history and others made by Tolstoy, this extraordinary novel takes on investigating the hypothesis of history and the irrelevance of noted figures like Alexander and Napoleon. Anna Karenina, Tolstoy's next epic was begun in 1873 and distributed totally in 1878.

Contents

BOOK ONE : 1805

CHAPTER I	9
CHAPTER II	15
CHAPTER III	19
CHAPTER IV	23
CHAPTER V	27
CHAPTER VI	33
CHAPTER VII	37
CHAPTER VIII	41
CHAPTER IX	45
CHAPTER X	51
CHAPTER XI	56
CHAPTER XII	59
CHAPTER XIII	63
CHAPTER XIV	66
CHAPTER XV	71
CHAPTER XVI	76
CHAPTER XVII	81
CHAPTER XVIII	84
CHAPTER XIX	90
CHAPTER XX	94
CHAPTER XXI	100
CHAPTER XXII	108
CHAPTER XXIII	113
CHAPTER XXIV	118
CHAPTER XXV	123
CHAPTER XXVI	132
CHAPTER XXVII	138
CHAPTER XXVIII	143

BOOK ONE : 1805

CHAPTER I

"Well, Prince, so Genoa and Lucca are now just family estates of the Buonapartes. But I warn you, if you don't tell me that this means war, if you still try to defend the infamies and horrors perpetrated by that Antichrist—I really believe he is Antichrist—I will have nothing more to do with you and you are no longer my friend, no longer my 'faithful slave,' as you call yourself! But how do you do? I see I have frightened you—sit down and tell me all the news."

It was in July, 1805, and the speaker was the well-known Anna PávlovnaSchérer, maid of honor and favorite of the Empress MáryaFëdorovna. With these words she greeted Prince VasíliKurágin, a man of high rank and importance, who was the first to arrive at her reception. Anna Pávlovna had had a cough for some days. She was, as she said, suffering from *la grippe; grippe* being then a new word in St. Petersburg, used only by the elite.

All her invitations without exception, written in French, and delivered by a scarlet-liveried footman that morning, ran as follows:

"If you have nothing better to do, Count (or Prince), and if the prospect of spending an evening with a poor invalid is not too terrible, I shall be very charmed to see you tonight between 7 and 10—Annette Schérer."

"Heavens! what a virulent attack!" replied the prince, not in the least disconcerted by this reception. He had just entered, wearing an embroidered court uniform, knee breeches, and shoes, and had stars on his breast and a serene expression on his flat face. He spoke in that refined French in which our grandfathers not only spoke but thought, and with the gentle, patronizing intonation natural to a man of importance who had grown old in society and at court. He went up to Anna Pávlovna, kissed her hand, presenting to her his bald, scented, and shining head, and complacently seated himself on the sofa.

"First of all, dear friend, tell me how you are. Set your friend's mind at rest," said he without altering his tone, beneath the politeness and affected sympathy of which indifference and even irony could be discerned.

"Can one be well while suffering morally? Can one be calm in times like these if one has any feeling?" said Anna Pávlovna. "You are staying the whole evening, I hope?"

"And the fete at the English ambassador's? Today is Wednesday. I must put in an appearance there," said the prince. "My daughter is coming for me to take me there."

"I thought today's fete had been canceled. I confess all these festivities and fireworks are becoming wearisome."

"If they had known that you wished it, the entertainment would have been put off," said the prince, who, like a wound-up clock, by force of habit said things he did not even wish to be believed.

"Don't tease! Well, and what has been decided about Novosíltsev's dispatch? You know everything."

"What can one say about it?" replied the prince in a cold, listless tone. "What has been decided? They have decided that Buonaparte has burnt his boats, and I believe that we are ready to burn ours."

Prince Vasíli always spoke languidly, like an actor repeating a stale part. Anna PávlovnaSchérer on the contrary, despite her forty years, overflowed with animation and impulsiveness. To be an enthusiast had become her social vocation and, sometimes even when she did not feel like it, she became enthusiastic in order not to disappoint the expectations of those who knew her. The subdued smile which, though it did not suit her faded features, always played round her lips expressed, as in a spoiled child, a continual consciousness of her charming defect, which she neither wished, nor could, nor considered it necessary, to correct.

In the midst of a conversation on political matters Anna Pávlovna burst out:

"Oh, don't speak to me of Austria. Perhaps I don't understand things, but Austria never has wished, and does not wish, for war. She is betraying us! Russia alone must save Europe. Our gracious sovereign recognizes his high vocation and will be true to it. That is the one thing I have faith in! Our good and wonderful sovereign has to perform the noblest role on earth, and he is so virtuous and noble that God will not forsake him. He will fulfill his vocation and crush the hydra of revolution, which has become more terrible than ever in the person of this murderer and villain! We alone must avenge the blood of the just one.... Whom, I ask you, can we rely on?... England with her commercial spirit will not and cannot understand the Emperor Alexander's loftiness of soul. She has refused to evacuate Malta. She wanted to find, and still seeks, some secret motive in our actions. What answer did Novosíltsev get? None. The English have not understood and cannot understand the self-abnegation of our Emperor who wants nothing for himself, but only desires the good of mankind. And what have they promised? Nothing! And what little they have promised they will not perform! Prussia has always declared that Buonaparte is invincible, and that all Europe is powerless before him.... And I don't believe a word that Hardenburg says, or Haugwitz either. This famous Prussian neutrality is just a trap. I have faith only in God and the lofty destiny of our adored monarch. He will save Europe!"

She suddenly paused, smiling at her own impetuosity.

"I think," said the prince with a smile, "that if you had been sent instead of our dear Wintzingerode you would have captured the King of Prussia's consent by assault. You are so eloquent. Will you give me a cup of tea?"

"In a moment. À propos," she added, becoming calm again, "I am expecting two very interesting men tonight, le Vicomte de Mortemart, who is connected with the Montmorencys through the Rohans, one of the best French families. He is one of the genuine *émigrés*, the good ones. And also the Abbé Morio. Do you know that profound thinker? He has been received by the Emperor. Had you heard?"

"I shall be delighted to meet them," said the prince. "But tell me," he added with studied carelessness as if it had only just occurred to him, though the question he was about to ask was the chief motive of his visit, "is it true that the Dowager Empress wants Baron Funke to be appointed first secretary at Vienna? The baron by all accounts is a poor creature."

Prince Vasíli wished to obtain this post for his son, but others were trying through the Dowager Empress MáryaFëdorovna to secure it for the baron.

Anna Pávlovna almost closed her eyes to indicate that neither she nor anyone else had a right to criticize what the Empress desired or was pleased with.

"Baron Funke has been recommended to the Dowager Empress by her sister," was all she said, in a dry and mournful tone.

As she named the Empress, Anna Pávlovna's face suddenly assumed an expression of profound and sincere devotion and respect mingled with sadness, and this occurred every time she mentioned her illustrious patroness. She added that Her Majesty had deigned to show Baron Funke *beaucoup d'estime*, and again her face clouded over with sadness.

The prince was silent and looked indifferent. But, with the womanly and courtierlike quickness and tact habitual to her, Anna Pávlovna wished both to rebuke him (for daring to speak as he had done of a man recommended to the Empress) and at the same time to console him, so she said:

"Now about your family. Do you know that since your daughter came out everyone has been enraptured by her? They say she is amazingly beautiful."

The prince bowed to signify his respect and gratitude.

"I often think," she continued after a short pause, drawing nearer to the prince and smiling amiably at him as if to show that political and social topics were ended and the time had come for intimate conversation—"I often think how unfairly sometimes the joys of life are distributed. Why has fate given you two such splendid children? I don't speak of Anatole, your youngest. I don't like him," she added in a tone admitting of no rejoinder and raising her eyebrows. "Two such charming children. And really you appreciate them less than anyone, and so you don't deserve to have them."

And she smiled her ecstatic smile.

"I can't help it," said the prince. "Lavater would have said I lack the bump of paternity."

"Don't joke; I mean to have a serious talk with you. Do you know I am dissatisfied with your younger son? Between ourselves" (and her face assumed its melancholy expression), "he was mentioned at Her Majesty's and you were pitied...."

The prince answered nothing, but she looked at him significantly, awaiting a reply. He frowned.

"What would you have me do?" he said at last. "You know I did all a father could for their education, and they have both turned out fools. Hippolyte is at least a quiet fool, but Anatole is an active one. That is the only difference between them." He said this smiling in a way more natural and animated than usual, so that the wrinkles round his mouth very clearly revealed something unexpectedly coarse and unpleasant.

"And why are children born to such men as you? If you were not a father there would be nothing I could reproach you with," said Anna Pávlovna, looking up pensively.

"I am your faithful slave and to you alone I can confess that my children are the bane of my life. It is the cross I have to bear. That is how I explain it to myself. It can't be helped!"

He said no more, but expressed his resignation to cruel fate by a gesture. Anna Pávlovna meditated.

"Have you never thought of marrying your prodigal son Anatole?" she asked. "They say old maids have a mania for matchmaking, and though I don't feel that weakness in myself as yet, I know a little person who is very unhappy with her father. She is a relation of yours, Princess Mary Bolkónskaya."

Prince Vasíli did not reply, though, with the quickness of memory and perception befitting a man of the world, he indicated by a movement of the head that he was considering this information.

"Do you know," he said at last, evidently unable to check the sad current of his thoughts, "that Anatole is costing me forty thousand rubles a year? And," he went on after a pause, "what will it be in five years, if he goes on like this?" Presently he added: "That's what we fathers have to put up with.... Is this princess of yours rich?"

"Her father is very rich and stingy. He lives in the country. He is the well-known Prince Bolkónski who had to retire from the army under the late Emperor, and was nicknamed 'the King of Prussia.' He is very clever but eccentric, and a bore. The poor girl is very unhappy. She has a brother; I think you know him, he married Lise Meinen lately. He is an aide-de-camp of Kutúzov's and will be here tonight."

"Listen, dear Annette," said the prince, suddenly taking Anna Pávlovna's hand and for some reason drawing it downwards. "Arrange that affair for me and I shall always be your most devoted slave-*slafe* with an *f*, as a village elder of mine writes in his reports. She is rich and of good family and that's all I want."

And with the familiarity and easy grace peculiar to him, he raised the maid of honor's hand to his lips, kissed it, and swung it to and fro as he lay back in his armchair, looking in another direction.

"*Attendez*," said Anna Pávlovna, reflecting, "I'll speak to Lise, young Bolkónski's wife, this very evening, and perhaps the thing can be arranged. It shall be on your family's behalf that I'll start my apprenticeship as old maid."

CHAPTER II

Anna Pávlovna's drawing room was gradually filling. The highest Petersburg society was assembled there: people differing widely in age and character but alike in the social circle to which they belonged. Prince Vasíli's daughter, the beautiful Hélène, came to take her father to the ambassador's entertainment; she wore a ball dress and her badge as maid of honor. The youthful little Princess Bolkónskaya, known as *la femme la plus séduisante de Pétersbourg*,* was also there. She had been married during the previous winter, and being pregnant did not go to any large gatherings, but only to small receptions. Prince Vasíli's son, Hippolyte, had come with Mortemart, whom he introduced. The Abbé Morio and many others had also come.

* The most fascinating woman in Petersburg.

To each new arrival Anna Pávlovna said, "You have not yet seen my aunt," or "You do not know my aunt?" and very gravely conducted him or her to a little old lady, wearing large bows of ribbon in her cap, who had come sailing in from another room as soon as the guests began to arrive; and slowly turning her eyes from the visitor to her aunt, Anna Pávlovna mentioned each one's name and then left them.

Each visitor performed the ceremony of greeting this old aunt whom not one of them knew, not one of them wanted to know, and not one of them cared about; Anna Pávlovna observed these greetings with mournful and solemn interest and silent approval. The aunt spoke to each of them in the same words, about their health and her own, and the health of Her Majesty, "who, thank God, was better today." And each visitor, though politeness prevented his showing impatience, left the old woman with a sense of relief at having performed a vexatious duty and did not return to her the whole evening.

The young Princess Bolkónskaya had brought some work in a gold-embroidered velvet bag. Her pretty little upper lip, on which a delicate dark down was just perceptible, was too short for her teeth, but it lifted all the more sweetly, and was especially charming when she occasionally drew it down to meet the lower lip. As is always the case with a thoroughly attractive woman, her defect—the shortness of her upper lip and her half-open mouth—seemed to be her own special and peculiar form of beauty. Everyone brightened at the sight of this pretty young woman, so soon to become a mother, so full of life and health, and carrying her burden so lightly. Old men and dull dispirited young ones who looked at her, after being in her company and talking to her a little while, felt as if they too were becoming, like her, full of life and health. All who talked to her, and at each word saw her bright smile and the constant gleam of her white teeth, thought that they were in a specially amiable mood that day.

The little princess went round the table with quick, short, swaying steps, her workbag on her arm, and gaily spreading out her dress sat down on a sofa near the silver samovar, as if all she was doing was a pleasure to herself and to all around her. "I have brought my work," said she in French, displaying her bag and addressing all present. "Mind, Annette, I hope you have not played a wicked trick on me," she added, turning to her hostess. "You wrote that it was to be quite a small reception, and just see how badly I am dressed." And she spread out her arms to show her short-waisted, lace-trimmed, dainty gray dress, girdled with a broad ribbon just below the breast.

"*Soyeztranquille, Lise,* you will always be prettier than anyone else," replied Anna Pávlovna.

"You know," said the princess in the same tone of voice and still in French, turning to a general, "my husband is deserting me? He is going to get himself killed. Tell me what this wretched war is for?" she added, addressing Prince Vasíli, and without waiting for an answer she turned to speak to his daughter, the beautiful Hélène.

"What a delightful woman this little princess is!" said Prince Vasíli to Anna Pávlovna.

One of the next arrivals was a stout, heavily built young man with close-cropped hair, spectacles, the light-colored breeches fashionable at that time, a very high ruffle, and a brown dress coat. This stout young man was an illegitimate son of Count Bezúkhov, a well-known grandee of Catherine's time who now lay dying in Moscow. The young man had not yet entered either the military or civil service, as he had only just returned from abroad where he had been educated, and this was his first appearance in society. Anna Pávlovna greeted him with the nod she accorded to the lowest hierarchy in her drawing room. But in spite of this lowest-grade greeting, a look of anxiety and fear, as at the sight of something too large and unsuited to the place, came over her face when she saw Pierre enter. Though he was certainly rather bigger than the other men in the room, her anxiety could only have reference to the clever though shy, but observant and natural, expression which distinguished him from everyone else in that drawing room.

"It is very good of you, Monsieur Pierre, to come and visit a poor invalid," said Anna Pávlovna, exchanging an alarmed glance with her aunt as she conducted him to her.

Pierre murmured something unintelligible, and continued to look round as if in search of something. On his way to the aunt he bowed to the little princess with a pleased smile, as to an intimate acquaintance.

Anna Pávlovna's alarm was justified, for Pierre turned away from the aunt without waiting to hear her speech about Her Majesty's health. Anna Pávlovna in dismay detained him with the words: "Do you know the Abbé Morio? He is a most interesting man."

"Yes, I have heard of his scheme for perpetual peace, and it is very interesting but hardly feasible."

"You think so?" rejoined Anna Pávlovna in order to say something and get away to attend to her duties as hostess. But Pierre now committed a reverse act of impoliteness. First he had left a lady before she had finished speaking to him, and now he continued to speak to another who wished to get away. With his head bent, and his big feet spread apart, he began explaining his reasons for thinking the abbé's plan chimerical.

"We will talk of it later," said Anna Pávlovna with a smile.

And having got rid of this young man who did not know how to behave, she resumed her duties as hostess and continued to listen and watch, ready to help at any point where the conversation might happen to flag. As the foreman of a spinning mill, when he has set the hands to work, goes round and notices here a spindle that has stopped or there one that creaks or makes more noise than it should, and hastens to check the machine or set it in proper motion, so Anna Pávlovna moved about her drawing room, approaching now a silent, now a too-noisy group, and by a word or slight rearrangement kept the conversational machine in steady, proper, and regular motion. But amid these cares her anxiety about Pierre was evident. She kept an anxious watch on him when he approached the group round Mortemart to listen to what was being said there, and again when he passed to another group whose center was the abbé.

Pierre had been educated abroad, and this reception at Anna Pávlovna's was the first he had attended in Russia. He knew that all the intellectual lights of Petersburg were gathered there and, like a child in a toyshop, did not know which way to look, afraid of missing any clever conversation that was to be heard. Seeing the self-confident and refined expression on the faces of those present he was always expecting to hear something very profound. At last he came up to Morio. Here the conversation seemed interesting and he stood waiting for an opportunity to express his own views, as young people are fond of doing.

CHAPTER III

Anna Pávlovna's reception was in full swing. The spindles hummed steadily and ceaselessly on all sides. With the exception of the aunt, beside whom sat only one elderly lady, who with her thin careworn face was rather out of place in this brilliant society, the whole company had settled into three groups. One, chiefly masculine, had formed round the abbé. Another, of young people, was grouped round the beautiful Princess Hélène, Prince Vasíli's daughter, and the little Princess Bolkónskaya, very pretty and rosy, though rather too plump for her age. The third group was gathered round Mortemart and Anna Pávlovna.

The vicomte was a nice-looking young man with soft features and polished manners, who evidently considered himself a celebrity but out of politeness modestly placed himself at the disposal of the circle in which he found himself. Anna Pávlovna was obviously serving him up as a treat to her guests. As a clever maître d'hôtel serves up as a specially choice delicacy a piece of meat that no one who had seen it in the kitchen would have cared to eat, so Anna Pávlovna served up to her guests, first the vicomte and then the abbé, as peculiarly choice morsels. The group about Mortemart immediately began discussing the murder of the Duc d'Enghien. The vicomte said that the Duc d'Enghien had perished by his own magnanimity, and that there were particular reasons for Buonaparte's hatred of him.

"Ah, yes! Do tell us all about it, Vicomte," said Anna Pávlovna, with a pleasant feeling that there was something *à la Louis XV* in the sound of that sentence: *"Contez nous çela, Vicomte."*

The vicomte bowed and smiled courteously in token of his willingness to comply. Anna Pávlovna arranged a group round him, inviting everyone to listen to his tale.

"The vicomte knew the duc personally," whispered Anna Pávlovna to one of the guests. "The vicomte is a wonderful raconteur," said she to another. "How evidently he belongs to the best society," said she to a third; and the vicomte was served up to the company in the choicest and most advantageous style, like a well-garnished joint of roast beef on a hot dish.

The vicomte wished to begin his story and gave a subtle smile.

"Come over here, Hélène, dear," said Anna Pávlovna to the beautiful young princess who was sitting some way off, the center of another group.

The princess smiled. She rose with the same unchanging smile with which she had first entered the room—the smile of a perfectly beautiful woman. With a slight rustle of her white dress trimmed with moss and ivy, with a gleam of white shoulders, glossy hair, and sparkling diamonds, she passed between the men who made way for her, not looking at any of them but smiling on all, as if graciously allowing each the privilege of admiring her beautiful figure and shapely shoulders, back, and bosom—which in the fashion of those days were very much exposed—and she seemed to bring the glamour of a ballroom with her as she moved toward Anna Pávlovna. Hélène was so lovely that not only did she not show any trace of coquetry, but on the contrary she even appeared shy of her unquestionable and all too victorious beauty. She seemed to wish, but to be unable, to diminish its effect.

"How lovely!" said everyone who saw her; and the vicomte lifted his shoulders and dropped his eyes as if startled by something extraordinary when she took her seat opposite and beamed upon him also with her unchanging smile.

"Madame, I doubt my ability before such an audience," said he, smilingly inclining his head.

The princess rested her bare round arm on a little table and considered a reply unnecessary. She smilingly waited. All the time the story was being told she sat upright, glancing now at her beautiful round arm, altered in shape by its pressure on the table, now at her still more beautiful bosom, on which she readjusted a diamond necklace. From time to time she smoothed the folds of her dress, and whenever the story produced an effect she glanced at Anna Pávlovna, at once adopted just the expression she saw on the maid of honor's face, and again relapsed into her radiant smile.

The little princess had also left the tea table and followed Hélène. "Wait a moment, I'll get my work.... Now then, what are you thinking of?" she went on, turning to Prince Hippolyte. "Fetch me my workbag."

There was a general movement as the princess, smiling and talking merrily to everyone at once, sat down and gaily arranged herself in her seat.

"Now I am all right," she said, and asking the vicomte to begin, she took up her work.

Prince Hippolyte, having brought the workbag, joined the circle and moving a chair close to hers seated himself beside her.

Le charmant Hippolyte was surprising by his extraordinary resemblance to his beautiful sister, but yet more by the fact that in spite of this resemblance he was exceedingly ugly. His features were like his sister's, but while in her case everything was lit up by a joyous, self-satisfied, youthful, and constant smile of animation, and by the wonderful classic beauty of her figure, his face on the contrary was dulled by imbecility and a constant expression of sullen self-confidence, while his body was thin and weak. His eyes, nose, and mouth all seemed puckered into a vacant, wearied grimace, and his arms and legs always fell into unnatural positions.

"It's not going to be a ghost story?" said he, sitting down beside the princess and hastily adjusting his lorgnette, as if without this instrument he could not begin to speak.

"Why no, my dear fellow," said the astonished narrator, shrugging his shoulders.

"Because I hate ghost stories," said Prince Hippolyte in a tone which showed that he only understood the meaning of his words after he had uttered them.

He spoke with such self-confidence that his hearers could not be sure whether what he said was very witty or very stupid. He was dressed in a dark-green dress coat, knee breeches of the color of *cuisse de nympheeffrayée*, as he called it, shoes, and silk stockings.

The vicomte told his tale very neatly. It was an anecdote, then current, to the effect that the Duc d'Enghien had gone secretly to Paris to visit Mademoiselle George; that at her house he came upon Bonaparte, who also enjoyed the famous actress' favors, and that in his presence Napoleon happened to fall into one of the fainting fits to which he was subject, and was thus at the duc's mercy. The latter spared him, and this magnanimity Bonaparte subsequently repaid by death.

The story was very pretty and interesting, especially at the point where the rivals suddenly recognized one another; and the ladies looked agitated.

"Charming!" said Anna Pávlovna with an inquiring glance at the little princess.

"Charming!" whispered the little princess, sticking the needle into her work as if to testify that the interest and fascination of the story prevented her from going on with it.

The vicomte appreciated this silent praise and smiling gratefully prepared to continue, but just then Anna Pávlovna, who had kept a watchful eye on the young man who so alarmed her, noticed that he was talking too loudly and vehemently with the abbé, so she hurried to the rescue. Pierre had managed to start a conversation with the abbé about the balance of power, and the latter, evidently interested by the young man's simple-minded eagerness, was explaining his pet theory. Both were talking and listening too eagerly and too naturally, which was why Anna Pávlovna disapproved.

"The means are ... the balance of power in Europe and the rights of the people," the abbé was saying. "It is only necessary for one powerful nation like Russia—barbaric as she is said to be—to place herself disinterestedly at the head of an alliance having for its object the maintenance of the balance of power of Europe, and it would save the world!"

"But how are you to get that balance?" Pierre was beginning.

At that moment Anna Pávlovna came up and, looking severely at Pierre, asked the Italian how he stood Russian climate. The Italian's face instantly changed and assumed an offensively affected, sugary expression, evidently habitual to him when conversing with women.

"I am so enchanted by the brilliancy of the wit and culture of the society, more especially of the feminine society, in which I have had the honor of being received, that I have not yet had time to think of the climate," said he.

Not letting the abbé and Pierre escape, Anna Pávlovna, the more conveniently to keep them under observation, brought them into the larger circle.

CHAPTER IV

Just then another visitor entered the drawing room: Prince Andrew Bolkónski, the little princess' husband. He was a very handsome young man, of medium height, with firm, clearcut features. Everything about him, from his weary, bored expression to his quiet, measured step, offered a most striking contrast to his quiet, little wife. It was evident that he not only knew everyone in the drawing room, but had found them to be so tiresome that it wearied him to look at or listen to them. And among all these faces that he found so tedious, none seemed to bore him so much as that of his pretty wife. He turned away from her with a grimace that distorted his handsome face, kissed Anna Pávlovna's hand, and screwing up his eyes scanned the whole company.

"You are off to the war, Prince?" said Anna Pávlovna.

"General Kutúzov," said Bolkónski, speaking French and stressing the last syllable of the general's name like a Frenchman, "has been pleased to take me as an aide-de-camp...."

"And Lise, your wife?"

"She will go to the country."

"Are you not ashamed to deprive us of your charming wife?"

"André," said his wife, addressing her husband in the same coquettish manner in which she spoke to other men, "the vicomte has been telling us such a tale about Mademoiselle George and Buonaparte!"

Prince Andrew screwed up his eyes and turned away. Pierre, who from the moment Prince Andrew entered the room had watched him with glad, affectionate eyes, now came up and took his arm. Before he looked round Prince Andrew frowned again, expressing his annoyance with whoever was touching his arm, but when he saw Pierre's beaming face he gave him an unexpectedly kind and pleasant smile.

"There now!... So you, too, are in the great world?" said he to Pierre.

"I knew you would be here," replied Pierre. "I will come to supper with you. May I?" he added in a low voice so as not to disturb the vicomte who was continuing his story.

"No, impossible!" said Prince Andrew, laughing and pressing Pierre's hand to show that there was no need to ask the question. He wished to say something more, but at that moment Prince Vasíli and his daughter got up to go and the two young men rose to let them pass.

"You must excuse me, dear Vicomte," said Prince Vasíli to the Frenchman, holding him down by the sleeve in a friendly way to prevent his rising. "This unfortunate fete at the ambassador's deprives me of a pleasure, and obliges me to interrupt you. I am very sorry to leave your enchanting party," said he, turning to Anna Pávlovna.

His daughter, Princess Hélène, passed between the chairs, lightly holding up the folds of her dress, and the smile shone still more radiantly on her beautiful face. Pierre gazed at her with rapturous, almost frightened, eyes as she passed him.

"Very lovely," said Prince Andrew.

"Very," said Pierre.

In passing Prince Vasíli seized Pierre's hand and said to Anna Pávlovna: "Educate this bear for me! He has been staying with me a whole month and this is the first time I have seen him in society. Nothing is so necessary for a young man as the society of clever women."

Anna Pávlovna smiled and promised to take Pierre in hand. She knew his father to be a connection of Prince Vasíli's. The elderly lady who had been sitting with the old aunt rose hurriedly and overtook Prince Vasíli in the anteroom. All the affectation of interest she had assumed had left her kindly and tear-worn face and it now expressed only anxiety and fear.

"How about my son Borís, Prince?" said she, hurrying after him into the anteroom. "I can't remain any longer in Petersburg. Tell me what news I may take back to my poor boy."

Although Prince Vasíli listened reluctantly and not very politely to the elderly lady, even betraying some impatience, she gave him an ingratiating and appealing smile, and took his hand that he might not go away.

"What would it cost you to say a word to the Emperor, and then he would be transferred to the Guards at once?" said she.

"Believe me, Princess, I am ready to do all I can," answered Prince Vasíli, "but it is difficult for me to ask the Emperor. I should advise you to appeal to Rumyántsev through Prince Golítsyn. That would be the best way."

The elderly lady was a Princess Drubetskáya, belonging to one of the best families in Russia, but she was poor, and having long been out of society had lost her former influential connections. She had now come to Petersburg to procure an appointment in the Guards for her only son. It was, in fact, solely to meet Prince Vasíli that she had obtained an invitation to Anna Pávlovna's reception and had sat listening to the vicomte's story. Prince Vasíli's words frightened her, an embittered look clouded her once handsome face, but only for a moment; then she smiled again and clutched Prince Vasíli's arm more tightly.

"Listen to me, Prince," said she. "I have never yet asked you for anything and I never will again, nor have I ever reminded you of my father's friendship for you; but now I entreat you for God's sake to do this for my son—and I shall always regard you as a benefactor," she added hurriedly. "No, don't be angry, but promise! I have asked Golítsyn and he has refused. Be the kindhearted man you always were," she said, trying to smile though tears were in her eyes.

"Papa, we shall be late," said Princess Hélène, turning her beautiful head and looking over her classically molded shoulder as she stood waiting by the door.

Influence in society, however, is a capital which has to be economized if it is to last. Prince Vasíli knew this, and having once realized that if he asked on behalf of all who begged of him, he would soon be unable to ask for himself, he became chary of using his influence. But in Princess Drubetskáya's case he felt, after her second appeal, something like qualms of conscience. She had reminded him of what was quite true; he had been indebted to her father for the first steps in his career. Moreover, he could see by her manners that she was one of those women—mostly mothers—who, having once made up their minds, will not rest until they have gained their end, and are prepared if necessary to go on insisting day after day and hour after hour, and even to make scenes. This last consideration moved him.

"My dear Anna Mikháylovna," said he with his usual familiarity and weariness of tone, "it is almost impossible for me to do what you ask; but to prove my devotion to you and how I respect your father's memory, I will do the impossible—your son shall be transferred to the Guards. Here is my hand on it. Are you satisfied?"

"My dear benefactor! This is what I expected from you—I knew your kindness!" He turned to go.

"Wait—just a word! When he has been transferred to the Guards..." she faltered. "You are on good terms with Michael IlariónovichKutúzov ... recommend Borís to him as adjutant! Then I shall be at rest, and then..."

Prince Vasíli smiled.

"No, I won't promise that. You don't know how Kutúzov is pestered since his appointment as Commander in Chief. He told me himself that all the Moscow ladies have conspired to give him all their sons as adjutants."

"No, but do promise! I won't let you go! My dear benefactor..."

"Papa," said his beautiful daughter in the same tone as before, "we shall be late."

"Well, *au revoir!* Good-by! You hear her?"

"Then tomorrow you will speak to the Emperor?"

"Certainly; but about Kutúzov, I don't promise."

"Do promise, do promise, Vasíli!" cried Anna Mikháylovna as he went, with the smile of a coquettish girl, which at one time probably came naturally to her, but was now very ill-suited to her careworn face.

Apparently she had forgotten her age and by force of habit employed all the old feminine arts. But as soon as the prince had gone her face resumed its former cold, artificial expression. She returned to the group where the vicomte was still talking, and again pretended to listen, while waiting till it would be time to leave. Her task was accomplished.

CHAPTER V

"And what do you think of this latest comedy, the coronation at Milan?" asked Anna Pávlovna, "and of the comedy of the people of Genoa and Lucca laying their petitions before Monsieur Buonaparte, and Monsieur Buonaparte sitting on a throne and granting the petitions of the nations? Adorable! It is enough to make one's head whirl! It is as if the whole world had gone crazy."

Prince Andrew looked Anna Pávlovna straight in the face with a sarcastic smile.

"*Dieu me la donne, gare à qui la touche!*" * They say he was very fine when he said that," he remarked, repeating the words in Italian: "*Dio mi l'hadato. Guai a chi la tocchi!*"

* God has given it to me, let him who touches it beware!

"I hope this will prove the last drop that will make the glass run over," Anna Pávlovna continued. "The sovereigns will not be able to endure this man who is a menace to everything."

"The sovereigns? I do not speak of Russia," said the vicomte, polite but hopeless: "The sovereigns, madame... What have they done for Louis XVII, for the Queen, or for Madame Elizabeth? Nothing!" and he became more animated. "And believe me, they are reaping the reward of their betrayal of the Bourbon cause. The sovereigns! Why, they are sending ambassadors to compliment the usurper."

And sighing disdainfully, he again changed his position.

Prince Hippolyte, who had been gazing at the vicomte for some time through his lorgnette, suddenly turned completely round toward the little princess, and having asked for a needle began tracing the Condé coat of arms on the table. He explained this to her with as much gravity as if she had asked him to do it.

"*Bâton de gueules, engrêlé de gueules d'azur—maison Condé,*" said he.

The princess listened, smiling.

"If Buonaparte remains on the throne of France a year longer," the vicomte continued, with the air of a man who, in a matter with which he is better acquainted than anyone else, does not listen to others but follows the current of his own thoughts, "things will have gone too far. By intrigues, violence, exile, and executions, French society—I mean good French society—will have been forever destroyed, and then...."

He shrugged his shoulders and spread out his hands. Pierre wished to make a remark, for the conversation interested him, but Anna Pávlovna, who had him under observation, interrupted:

"The Emperor Alexander," said she, with the melancholy which always accompanied any reference of hers to the Imperial family, "has declared that he will leave it to the French people themselves to choose their own form of government; and I believe that once free from the usurper, the whole nation will certainly throw itself into the arms of its rightful king," she concluded, trying to be amiable to the royalist emigrant.

"That is doubtful," said Prince Andrew. "Monsieur le Vicomte quite rightly supposes that matters have already gone too far. I think it will be difficult to return to the old regime."

"From what I have heard," said Pierre, blushing and breaking into the conversation, "almost all the aristocracy has already gone over to Bonaparte's side."

"It is the Buonapartists who say that," replied the vicomte without looking at Pierre. "At the present time it is difficult to know the real state of French public opinion."

"Bonaparte has said so," remarked Prince Andrew with a sarcastic smile.

It was evident that he did not like the vicomte and was aiming his remarks at him, though without looking at him.

"'I showed them the path to glory, but they did not follow it,'" Prince Andrew continued after a short silence, again quoting Napoleon's words. "'I opened my antechambers and they crowded in.' I do not know how far he was justified in saying so."

"Not in the least," replied the vicomte. "After the murder of the duc even the most partial ceased to regard him as a hero. If to some people," he went on, turning to Anna Pávlovna, "he ever was a hero, after the murder of the duc there was one martyr more in heaven and one hero less on earth."

Before Anna Pávlovna and the others had time to smile their appreciation of the vicomte's epigram, Pierre again broke into the conversation, and though Anna Pávlovna felt sure he would say something inappropriate, she was unable to stop him.

"The execution of the Duc d'Enghien," declared Monsieur Pierre, "was a political necessity, and it seems to me that Napoleon showed greatness of soul by not fearing to take on himself the whole responsibility of that deed."

"*Dieu! Mon Dieu!*" muttered Anna Pávlovna in a terrified whisper.

"What, Monsieur Pierre... Do you consider that assassination shows greatness of soul?" said the little princess, smiling and drawing her work nearer to her.

"Oh! Oh!" exclaimed several voices.

"Capital!" said Prince Hippolyte in English, and began slapping his knee with the palm of his hand.

The vicomte merely shrugged his shoulders. Pierre looked solemnly at his audience over his spectacles and continued.

"I say so," he continued desperately, "because the Bourbons fled from the Revolution leaving the people to anarchy, and Napoleon alone understood the Revolution and quelled it, and so for the general good, he could not stop short for the sake of one man's life."

"Won't you come over to the other table?" suggested Anna Pávlovna.

But Pierre continued his speech without heeding her.

"No," cried he, becoming more and more eager, "Napoleon is great because he rose superior to the Revolution, suppressed its abuses, preserved all that was good in it—equality of citizenship and freedom of speech and of the press—and only for that reason did he obtain power."

"Yes, if having obtained power, without availing himself of it to commit murder he had restored it to the rightful king, I should have called him a great man," remarked the vicomte.

"He could not do that. The people only gave him power that he might rid them of the Bourbons and because they saw that he was a great man. The Revolution was a grand thing!" continued Monsieur Pierre, betraying by this desperate and provocative proposition his extreme youth and his wish to express all that was in his mind.

"What? Revolution and regicide a grand thing?... Well, after that... But won't you come to this other table?" repeated Anna Pávlovna.

"Rousseau's *Contrat Social*," said the vicomte with a tolerant smile.

"I am not speaking of regicide, I am speaking about ideas."

"Yes: ideas of robbery, murder, and regicide," again interjected an ironical voice.

"Those were extremes, no doubt, but they are not what is most important. What is important are the rights of man, emancipation from prejudices, and equality of citizenship, and all these ideas Napoleon has retained in full force."

"Liberty and equality," said the vicomte contemptuously, as if at last deciding seriously to prove to this youth how foolish his words were, "high-sounding words which have long been discredited. Who does not love liberty and equality? Even our Saviour preached liberty and equality. Have people since the Revolution become happier? On the contrary. We wanted liberty, but Buonaparte has destroyed it."

Prince Andrew kept looking with an amused smile from Pierre to the vicomte and from the vicomte to their hostess. In the first moment of Pierre's outburst Anna Pávlovna, despite her social experience, was horror-struck. But when she saw that Pierre's sacrilegious words had not exasperated the vicomte, and had convinced herself that it was impossible to stop him, she rallied her forces and joined the vicomte in a vigorous attack on the orator.

"But, my dear Monsieur Pierre," said she, "how do you explain the fact of a great man executing a duc—or even an ordinary man who—is innocent and untried?"

"I should like," said the vicomte, "to ask how monsieur explains the 18th Brumaire; was not that an imposture? It was a swindle, and not at all like the conduct of a great man!"

"And the prisoners he killed in Africa? That was horrible!" said the little princess, shrugging her shoulders.

"He's a low fellow, say what you will," remarked Prince Hippolyte.

Pierre, not knowing whom to answer, looked at them all and smiled. His smile was unlike the half-smile of other people. When he smiled, his grave, even rather gloomy, look was instantaneously replaced by another—a childlike, kindly, even rather silly look, which seemed to ask forgiveness.

The vicomte who was meeting him for the first time saw clearly that this young Jacobin was not so terrible as his words suggested. All were silent.

"How do you expect him to answer you all at once?" said Prince Andrew. "Besides, in the actions of a statesman one has to distinguish between his acts as a private person, as a general, and as an emperor. So it seems to me."

"Yes, yes, of course!" Pierre chimed in, pleased at the arrival of this reinforcement.

"One must admit," continued Prince Andrew, "that Napoleon as a man was great on the bridge of Arcola, and in the hospital at Jaffa where he gave his hand to the plague-stricken; but ... but there are other acts which it is difficult to justify."

Prince Andrew, who had evidently wished to tone down the awkwardness of Pierre's remarks, rose and made a sign to his wife that it was time to go.

Suddenly Prince Hippolyte started up making signs to everyone to attend, and asking them all to be seated began:

"I was told a charming Moscow story today and must treat you to it. Excuse me, Vicomte—I must tell it in Russian or the point will be lost...." And Prince Hippolyte began to tell his story in such Russian as a Frenchman would speak after spending about a year in Russia. Everyone waited, so emphatically and eagerly did he demand their attention to his story.

"There is in Moscow a lady, *une dame*, and she is very stingy. She must have two footmen behind her carriage, and very big ones. That was her taste. And she had a lady's maid, also big. She said...."

Here Prince Hippolyte paused, evidently collecting his ideas with difficulty.

"She said.... Oh yes! She said, 'Girl,' to the maid, 'put on a livery, get up behind the carriage, and come with me while I make some calls.'"

Here Prince Hippolyte spluttered and burst out laughing long before his audience, which produced an effect unfavorable to the narrator. Several persons, among them the elderly lady and Anna Pávlovna, did however smile.

"She went. Suddenly there was a great wind. The girl lost her hat and her long hair came down...." Here he could contain himself no longer and went on, between gasps of laughter: "And the whole world knew...."

And so the anecdote ended. Though it was unintelligible why he had told it, or why it had to be told in Russian, still Anna Pávlovna and the others appreciated Prince Hippolyte's social tact in so agreeably ending Pierre's unpleasant and unamiable outburst. After the anecdote the conversation broke up into insignificant small talk about the last and next balls, about theatricals, and who would meet whom, and when and where.

CHAPTER VI

Having thanked Anna Pávlovna for her charming soiree, the guests began to take their leave.

Pierre was ungainly. Stout, about the average height, broad, with huge red hands; he did not know, as the saying is, how to enter a drawing room and still less how to leave one; that is, how to say something particularly agreeable before going away. Besides this he was absent-minded. When he rose to go, he took up instead of his own, the general's three-cornered hat, and held it, pulling at the plume, till the general asked him to restore it. All his absent-mindedness and inability to enter a room and converse in it was, however, redeemed by his kindly, simple, and modest expression. Anna Pávlovna turned toward him and, with a Christian mildness that expressed forgiveness of his indiscretion, nodded and said: "I hope to see you again, but I also hope you will change your opinions, my dear Monsieur Pierre."

When she said this, he did not reply and only bowed, but again everybody saw his smile, which said nothing, unless perhaps, "Opinions are opinions, but you see what a capital, good-natured fellow I am." And everyone, including Anna Pávlovna, felt this.

Prince Andrew had gone out into the hall, and, turning his shoulders to the footman who was helping him on with his cloak, listened indifferently to his wife's chatter with Prince Hippolyte who had also come into the hall. Prince Hippolyte stood close to the pretty, pregnant princess, and stared fixedly at her through his eyeglass.

"Go in, Annette, or you will catch cold," said the little princess, taking leave of Anna Pávlovna. "It is settled," she added in a low voice.

Anna Pávlovna had already managed to speak to Lise about the match she contemplated between Anatole and the little princess' sister-in-law.

"I rely on you, my dear," said Anna Pávlovna, also in a low tone. "Write to her and let me know how her father looks at the matter. *Au revoir!*"—and she left the hall.

Prince Hippolyte approached the little princess and, bending his face close to her, began to whisper something.

Two footmen, the princess' and his own, stood holding a shawl and a cloak, waiting for the conversation to finish. They listened to the French sentences which to them were meaningless, with an air of understanding but not wishing to appear to do so. The princess as usual spoke smilingly and listened with a laugh.

"I am very glad I did not go to the ambassador's," said Prince Hippolyte "—so dull—. It has been a delightful evening, has it not? Delightful!"

"They say the ball will be very good," replied the princess, drawing up her downy little lip. "All the pretty women in society will be there."

"Not all, for you will not be there; not all," said Prince Hippolyte smiling joyfully; and snatching the shawl from the footman, whom he even pushed aside, he began wrapping it round the princess. Either from awkwardness or intentionally (no one could have said which) after the shawl had been adjusted he kept his arm around her for a long time, as though embracing her.

Still smiling, she gracefully moved away, turning and glancing at her husband. Prince Andrew's eyes were closed, so weary and sleepy did he seem.

"Are you ready?" he asked his wife, looking past her.

Prince Hippolyte hurriedly put on his cloak, which in the latest fashion reached to his very heels, and, stumbling in it, ran out into the porch following the princess, whom a footman was helping into the carriage.

"*Princesse, au revoir,*" cried he, stumbling with his tongue as well as with his feet.

The princess, picking up her dress, was taking her seat in the dark carriage, her husband was adjusting his saber; Prince Hippolyte, under pretense of helping, was in everyone's way.

"Allow me, sir," said Prince Andrew in Russian in a cold, disagreeable tone to Prince Hippolyte who was blocking his path.

"I am expecting you, Pierre," said the same voice, but gently and affectionately.

The postilion started, the carriage wheels rattled. Prince Hippolyte laughed spasmodically as he stood in the porch waiting for the vicomte whom he had promised to take home.

"Well, *moncher*," said the vicomte, having seated himself beside Hippolyte in the carriage, "your little princess is very nice, very nice indeed, quite French," and he kissed the tips of his fingers. Hippolyte burst out laughing.

"Do you know, you are a terrible chap for all your innocent airs," continued the vicomte. "I pity the poor husband, that little officer who gives himself the airs of a monarch."

Hippolyte spluttered again, and amid his laughter said, "And you were saying that the Russian ladies are not equal to the French? One has to know how to deal with them."

Pierre reaching the house first went into Prince Andrew's study like one quite at home, and from habit immediately lay down on the sofa, took from the shelf the first book that came to his hand (it was Caesar's *Commentaries*), and resting on his elbow, began reading it in the middle.

"What have you done to Mlle Schérer? She will be quite ill now," said Prince Andrew, as he entered the study, rubbing his small white hands.

Pierre turned his whole body, making the sofa creak. He lifted his eager face to Prince Andrew, smiled, and waved his hand.

"That abbé is very interesting but he does not see the thing in the right light.... In my opinion perpetual peace is possible but—I do not know how to express it ... not by a balance of political power...."

It was evident that Prince Andrew was not interested in such abstract conversation.

"One can't everywhere say all one thinks, *moncher*. Well, have you at last decided on anything? Are you going to be a guardsman or a diplomatist?" asked Prince Andrew after a momentary silence.

Pierre sat up on the sofa, with his legs tucked under him.

"Really, I don't yet know. I don't like either the one or the other."

"But you must decide on something! Your father expects it."

Pierre at the age of ten had been sent abroad with an abbé as tutor, and had remained away till he was twenty. When he returned to Moscow his father dismissed the abbé and said to the young man, "Now go to Petersburg, look round, and choose your profession. I will agree to anything. Here is a letter to Prince Vasíli, and here is money. Write to me all about it, and I will help you in everything." Pierre had already been choosing a career for three months, and had not decided on anything. It was about this choice that Prince Andrew was speaking. Pierre rubbed his forehead.

"But he must be a Freemason," said he, referring to the abbé whom he had met that evening.

"That is all nonsense." Prince Andrew again interrupted him, "let us talk business. Have you been to the Horse Guards?"

"No, I have not; but this is what I have been thinking and wanted to tell you. There is a war now against Napoleon. If it were a war for freedom I could understand it and should be the first to enter the army; but to help England and Austria against the greatest man in the world is not right."

Prince Andrew only shrugged his shoulders at Pierre's childish words. He put on the air of one who finds it impossible to reply to such nonsense, but it would in fact have been difficult to give any other answer than the one Prince Andrew gave to this naïve question.

"If no one fought except on his own conviction, there would be no wars," he said.

"And that would be splendid," said Pierre.

Prince Andrew smiled ironically.

"Very likely it would be splendid, but it will never come about...."

"Well, why are you going to the war?" asked Pierre.

"What for? I don't know. I must. Besides that I am going...." He paused. "I am going because the life I am leading here does not suit me!"

CHAPTER VII

The rustle of a woman's dress was heard in the next room. Prince Andrew shook himself as if waking up, and his face assumed the look it had had in Anna Pávlovna's drawing room. Pierre removed his feet from the sofa. The princess came in. She had changed her gown for a house dress as fresh and elegant as the other. Prince Andrew rose and politely placed a chair for her.

"How is it," she began, as usual in French, settling down briskly and fussily in the easy chair, "how is it Annette never got married? How stupid you men all are not to have married her! Excuse me for saying so, but you have no sense about women. What an argumentative fellow you are, Monsieur Pierre!"

"And I am still arguing with your husband. I can't understand why he wants to go to the war," replied Pierre, addressing the princess with none of the embarrassment so commonly shown by young men in their intercourse with young women.

The princess started. Evidently Pierre's words touched her to the quick.

"Ah, that is just what I tell him!" said she. "I don't understand it; I don't in the least understand why men can't live without wars. How is it that we women don't want anything of the kind, don't need it? Now you shall judge between us. I always tell him: Here he is Uncle's aide-de-camp, a most brilliant position. He is so well known, so much appreciated by everyone. The other day at the Apráksins' I heard a lady asking, 'Is that the famous Prince Andrew?' I did indeed." She laughed. "He is so well received everywhere. He might easily become aide-de-camp to the Emperor. You know the Emperor spoke to him most graciously. Annette and I were speaking of how to arrange it. What do you think?"

Pierre looked at his friend and, noticing that he did not like the conversation, gave no reply.

"When are you starting?" he asked.

"Oh, don't speak of his going, don't! I won't hear it spoken of," said the princess in the same petulantly playful tone in which she had spoken to Hippolyte in the drawing room and which was so plainly ill-suited to the family circle of which Pierre was almost a member. "Today when I remembered that all these delightful associations must be broken off ... and then you know, André..." (she looked significantly at her husband) "I'm afraid, I'm afraid!" she whispered, and a shudder ran down her back.

Her husband looked at her as if surprised to notice that someone besides Pierre and himself was in the room, and addressed her in a tone of frigid politeness.

"What is it you are afraid of, Lise? I don't understand," said he.

"There, what egotists men all are: all, all egotists! Just for a whim of his own, goodness only knows why, he leaves me and locks me up alone in the country."

"With my father and sister, remember," said Prince Andrew gently.

"Alone all the same, without *my* friends.... And he expects me not to be afraid."

Her tone was now querulous and her lip drawn up, giving her not a joyful, but an animal, squirrel-like expression. She paused as if she felt it indecorous to speak of her pregnancy before Pierre, though the gist of the matter lay in that.

"I still can't understand what you are afraid of," said Prince Andrew slowly, not taking his eyes off his wife.

The princess blushed, and raised her arms with a gesture of despair.

"No, Andrew, I must say you have changed. Oh, how you have...."

"Your doctor tells you to go to bed earlier," said Prince Andrew. "You had better go."

The princess said nothing, but suddenly her short downy lip quivered. Prince Andrew rose, shrugged his shoulders, and walked about the room.

Pierre looked over his spectacles with naïve surprise, now at him and now at her, moved as if about to rise too, but changed his mind.

"Why should I mind Monsieur Pierre being here?" exclaimed the little princess suddenly, her pretty face all at once distorted by a tearful grimace. "I have long wanted to ask you, Andrew, why you have changed so to me? What have I done to you? You are going to the war and have no pity for me. Why is it?"

"Lise!" was all Prince Andrew said. But that one word expressed an entreaty, a threat, and above all conviction that she would herself regret her words. But she went on hurriedly:

"You treat me like an invalid or a child. I see it all! Did you behave like that six months ago?"

"Lise, I beg you to desist," said Prince Andrew still more emphatically.

Pierre, who had been growing more and more agitated as he listened to all this, rose and approached the princess. He seemed unable to bear the sight of tears and was ready to cry himself.

"Calm yourself, Princess! It seems so to you because.... I assure you I myself have experienced ... and so ... because ... No, excuse me! An outsider is out of place here.... No, don't distress yourself.... Good-by!"

Prince Andrew caught him by the hand.

"No, wait, Pierre! The princess is too kind to wish to deprive me of the pleasure of spending the evening with you."

"No, he thinks only of himself," muttered the princess without restraining her angry tears.

War and Peace

"Lise!" said Prince Andrew dryly, raising his voice to the pitch which indicates that patience is exhausted.

Suddenly the angry, squirrel-like expression of the princess' pretty face changed into a winning and piteous look of fear. Her beautiful eyes glanced askance at her husband's face, and her own assumed the timid, deprecating expression of a dog when it rapidly but feebly wags its drooping tail.

"*Mon Dieu, mon Dieu!*" she muttered, and lifting her dress with one hand she went up to her husband and kissed him on the forehead.

"Good night, Lise," said he, rising and courteously kissing her hand as he would have done to a stranger.

CHAPTER VIII

The friends were silent. Neither cared to begin talking. Pierre continually glanced at Prince Andrew; Prince Andrew rubbed his forehead with his small hand.

"Let us go and have supper," he said with a sigh, going to the door.

They entered the elegant, newly decorated, and luxurious dining room. Everything from the table napkins to the silver, china, and glass bore that imprint of newness found in the households of the newly married. Halfway through supper Prince Andrew leaned his elbows on the table and, with a look of nervous agitation such as Pierre had never before seen on his face, began to talk—as one who has long had something on his mind and suddenly determines to speak out.

"Never, never marry, my dear fellow! That's my advice: never marry till you can say to yourself that you have done all you are capable of, and until you have ceased to love the woman of your choice and have seen her plainly as she is, or else you will make a cruel and irrevocable mistake. Marry when you are old and good for nothing—or all that is good and noble in you will be lost. It will all be wasted on trifles. Yes! Yes! Yes! Don't look at me with such surprise. If you marry expecting anything from yourself in the future, you will feel at every step that for you all is ended, all is closed except the drawing room, where you will be ranged side by side with a court lackey and an idiot!... But what's the good?..." and he waved his arm.

Pierre took off his spectacles, which made his face seem different and the good-natured expression still more apparent, and gazed at his friend in amazement.

"My wife," continued Prince Andrew, "is an excellent woman, one of those rare women with whom a man's honor is safe; but, O God, what would I not give now to be unmarried! You are the first and only one to whom I mention this, because I like you."

As he said this Prince Andrew was less than ever like that Bolkónski who had lolled in Anna Pávlovna's easy chairs and with half-closed eyes had uttered French phrases between his teeth. Every muscle of his thin face was now quivering with nervous excitement; his eyes, in which the fire of life had seemed extinguished, now flashed with brilliant light. It was evident that the more lifeless he seemed at ordinary times, the more impassioned he became in these moments of almost morbid irritation.

"You don't understand why I say this," he continued, "but it is the whole story of life. You talk of Bonaparte and his career," said he (though Pierre had not mentioned Bonaparte), "but Bonaparte when he worked went step by step toward his goal. He was free, he had nothing but his aim to consider, and he reached it. But tie yourself up with a woman and, like a chained convict, you lose all freedom! And all you have of hope and strength merely weighs you down and torments you with regret. Drawing rooms, gossip, balls, vanity, and triviality—these are the enchanted circle I cannot escape from. I am now going to the war, the greatest war there ever was, and I know nothing and am fit for nothing. I am very amiable and have a caustic wit," continued Prince Andrew, "and at Anna Pávlovna's they listen to me. And that stupid set without whom my wife cannot exist, and those women.... If you only knew what those society women are, and women in general! My father is right. Selfish, vain, stupid, trivial in everything—that's what women are when you see them in their true colors! When you meet them in society it seems as if there were something in them, but there's nothing, nothing, nothing! No, don't marry, my dear fellow; don't marry!" concluded Prince Andrew.

"It seems funny to me," said Pierre, "that *you, you* should consider yourself incapable and your life a spoiled life. You have everything before you, everything. And you...."

He did not finish his sentence, but his tone showed how highly he thought of his friend and how much he expected of him in the future.

"How can he talk like that?" thought Pierre. He considered his friend a model of perfection because Prince Andrew possessed in the highest degree just the very qualities Pierre lacked, and which might be best described as strength of will. Pierre was always astonished at Prince Andrew's calm manner of treating everybody, his extraordinary memory, his extensive reading (he had read everything, knew everything, and had an opinion about everything), but above all at his capacity for work and study. And if Pierre was often struck by Andrew's lack of capacity for philosophical meditation (to which he himself was particularly addicted), he regarded even this not as a defect but as a sign of strength.

Even in the best, most friendly and simplest relations of life, praise and commendation are essential, just as grease is necessary to wheels that they may run smoothly.

"My part is played out," said Prince Andrew. "What's the use of talking about me? Let us talk about you," he added after a silence, smiling at his reassuring thoughts.

That smile was immediately reflected on Pierre's face.

"But what is there to say about me?" said Pierre, his face relaxing into a careless, merry smile. "What am I? An illegitimate son!" He suddenly blushed crimson, and it was plain that he had made a great effort to say this. "Without a name and without means... And it really..." But he did not say what "it really" was. "For the present I am free and am all right. Only I haven't the least idea what I am to do; I wanted to consult you seriously."

Prince Andrew looked kindly at him, yet his glance—friendly and affectionate as it was—expressed a sense of his own superiority.

"I am fond of you, especially as you are the one live man among our whole set. Yes, you're all right! Choose what you will; it's all the same. You'll be all right anywhere. But look here: give up visiting those Kurágins and leading that sort of life. It suits you so badly—all this debauchery, dissipation, and the rest of it!"

"What would you have, my dear fellow?" answered Pierre, shrugging his shoulders. "Women, my dear fellow; women!"

"I don't understand it," replied Prince Andrew. "Women who are *comme il faut*, that's a different matter; but the Kurágins' set of women, 'women and wine' I don't understand!"

Pierre was staying at Prince VasíliKurágin's and sharing the dissipated life of his son Anatole, the son whom they were planning to reform by marrying him to Prince Andrew's sister.

"Do you know?" said Pierre, as if suddenly struck by a happy thought, "seriously, I have long been thinking of it.... Leading such a life I can't decide or think properly about anything. One's head aches, and one spends all one's money. He asked me for tonight, but I won't go."

"You give me your word of honor not to go?"

"On my honor!"

CHAPTER IX

It was past one o'clock when Pierre left his friend. It was a cloudless, northern, summer night. Pierre took an open cab intending to drive straight home. But the nearer he drew to the house the more he felt the impossibility of going to sleep on such a night. It was light enough to see a long way in the deserted street and it seemed more like morning or evening than night. On the way Pierre remembered that Anatole Kurágin was expecting the usual set for cards that evening, after which there was generally a drinking bout, finishing with visits of a kind Pierre was very fond of.

"I should like to go to Kurágin's," thought he.

But he immediately recalled his promise to Prince Andrew not to go there. Then, as happens to people of weak character, he desired so passionately once more to enjoy that dissipation he was so accustomed to that he decided to go. The thought immediately occurred to him that his promise to Prince Andrew was of no account, because before he gave it he had already promised Prince Anatole to come to his gathering; "besides," thought he, "all such 'words of honor' are conventional things with no definite meaning, especially if one considers that by tomorrow one may be dead, or something so extraordinary may happen to one that honor and dishonor will be all the same!" Pierre often indulged in reflections of this sort, nullifying all his decisions and intentions. He went to Kurágin's.

Reaching the large house near the Horse Guards' barracks, in which Anatole lived, Pierre entered the lighted porch, ascended the stairs, and went in at the open door. There was no one in the anteroom; empty bottles, cloaks, and overshoes were lying about; there was a smell of alcohol, and sounds of voices and shouting in the distance.

Cards and supper were over, but the visitors had not yet dispersed. Pierre threw off his cloak and entered the first room, in which were the remains of supper. A footman, thinking no one saw him, was drinking on the sly what was left in the glasses. From the third room came sounds of laughter, the shouting of familiar voices, the growling of a bear, and general commotion. Some eight or nine young men were crowding anxiously round an open window. Three others were romping with a young bear, one pulling him by the chain and trying to set him at the others.

"I bet a hundred on Stevens!" shouted one.

"Mind, no holding on!" cried another.

"I bet on Dólokhov!" cried a third. "Kurágin, you part our hands."

"There, leave Bruin alone; here's a bet on."

"At one draught, or he loses!" shouted a fourth.

"Jacob, bring a bottle!" shouted the host, a tall, handsome fellow who stood in the midst of the group, without a coat, and with his fine linen shirt unfastened in front. "Wait a bit, you fellows.... Here is Pétya! Good man!" cried he, addressing Pierre.

Another voice, from a man of medium height with clear blue eyes, particularly striking among all these drunken voices by its sober ring, cried from the window: "Come here; part the bets!" This was Dólokhov, an officer of the Semënov regiment, a notorious gambler and duelist, who was living with Anatole. Pierre smiled, looking about him merrily.

"I don't understand. What's it all about?"

"Wait a bit, he is not drunk yet! A bottle here," said Anatole, and taking a glass from the table he went up to Pierre.

"First of all you must drink!"

Pierre drank one glass after another, looking from under his brows at the tipsy guests who were again crowding round the window, and listening to their chatter. Anatole kept on refilling Pierre's glass while explaining that Dólokhov was betting with Stevens, an English naval officer, that he would drink a bottle of rum sitting on the outer ledge of the third floor window with his legs hanging out.

"Go on, you must drink it all," said Anatole, giving Pierre the last glass, "or I won't let you go!"

"No, I won't," said Pierre, pushing Anatole aside, and he went up to the window.

Dólokhov was holding the Englishman's hand and clearly and distinctly repeating the terms of the bet, addressing himself particularly to Anatole and Pierre.

Dólokhov was of medium height, with curly hair and light-blue eyes. He was about twenty-five. Like all infantry officers he wore no mustache, so that his mouth, the most striking feature of his face, was clearly seen. The lines of that mouth were remarkably finely curved. The middle of the upper lip formed a sharp wedge and closed firmly on the firm lower one, and something like two distinct smiles played continually round the two corners of the mouth; this, together with the resolute, insolent intelligence of his eyes, produced an effect which made it impossible not to notice his face. Dólokhov was a man of small means and no connections. Yet, though Anatole spent tens of thousands of rubles, Dólokhov lived with him and had placed himself on such a footing that all who knew them, including Anatole himself, respected him more than they did Anatole. Dólokhov could play all games and nearly always won. However much he drank, he never lost his clearheadedness. Both Kurágin and Dólokhov were at that time notorious among the rakes and scapegraces of Petersburg.

The bottle of rum was brought. The window frame which prevented anyone from sitting on the outer sill was being forced out by two footmen, who were evidently flurried and intimidated by the directions and shouts of the gentlemen around.

Anatole with his swaggering air strode up to the window. He wanted to smash something. Pushing away the footmen he tugged at the frame, but could not move it. He smashed a pane.

"You have a try, Hercules," said he, turning to Pierre.

Pierre seized the crossbeam, tugged, and wrenched the oak frame out with a crash.

"Take it right out, or they'll think I'm holding on," said Dólokhov.

"Is the Englishman bragging?... Eh? Is it all right?" said Anatole.

"First-rate," said Pierre, looking at Dólokhov, who with a bottle of rum in his hand was approaching the window, from which the light of the sky, the dawn merging with the afterglow of sunset, was visible.

Dólokhov, the bottle of rum still in his hand, jumped onto the window sill. "Listen!" cried he, standing there and addressing those in the room. All were silent.

"I bet fifty imperials"—he spoke French that the Englishman might understand him, but he did not speak it very well—"I bet fifty imperials ... or do you wish to make it a hundred?" added he, addressing the Englishman.

"No, fifty," replied the latter.

"All right. Fifty imperials ... that I will drink a whole bottle of rum without taking it from my mouth, sitting outside the window on this spot" (he stooped and pointed to the sloping ledge outside the window) "and without holding on to anything. Is that right?"

"Quite right," said the Englishman.

Anatole turned to the Englishman and taking him by one of the buttons of his coat and looking down at him—the Englishman was short—began repeating the terms of the wager to him in English.

"Wait!" cried Dólokhov, hammering with the bottle on the window sill to attract attention. "Wait a bit, Kurágin. Listen! If anyone else does the same, I will pay him a hundred imperials. Do you understand?"

The Englishman nodded, but gave no indication whether he intended to accept this challenge or not. Anatole did not release him, and though he kept nodding to show that he understood, Anatole went on translating Dólokhov's words into English. A thin young lad, an hussar of the Life Guards, who had been losing that evening, climbed on the window sill, leaned over, and looked down.

"Oh! Oh! Oh!" he muttered, looking down from the window at the stones of the pavement.

"Shut up!" cried Dólokhov, pushing him away from the window. The lad jumped awkwardly back into the room, tripping over his spurs.

Placing the bottle on the window sill where he could reach it easily, Dólokhov climbed carefully and slowly through the window and lowered his legs. Pressing against both sides of the window, he adjusted himself on his seat, lowered his hands, moved a little to the right and then to the left, and took up the bottle. Anatole brought two candles and placed them on the window sill, though it was already quite light. Dólokhov's back in his white shirt, and his curly head, were lit up from both sides. Everyone crowded to the window, the Englishman in front. Pierre stood smiling but silent. One man, older than the others present, suddenly pushed forward with a scared and angry look and wanted to seize hold of Dólokhov's shirt.

"I say, this is folly! He'll be killed," said this more sensible man.

Anatole stopped him.

"Don't touch him! You'll startle him and then he'll be killed. Eh?... What then?... Eh?"

Dólokhov turned round and, again holding on with both hands, arranged himself on his seat.

"If anyone comes meddling again," said he, emitting the words separately through his thin compressed lips, "I will throw him down there. Now then!"

Saying this he again turned round, dropped his hands, took the bottle and lifted it to his lips, threw back his head, and raised his free hand to balance himself. One of the footmen who had stooped to pick up some broken glass remained in that position without taking his eyes from the window and from Dólokhov's back. Anatole stood erect with staring eyes. The Englishman looked on sideways, pursing up his lips. The man who had wished to stop the affair ran to a corner of the room and threw himself on a sofa with his face to the wall. Pierre hid his face, from which a faint smile forgot to fade though his features now expressed horror and fear. All were still. Pierre took his hands from his eyes. Dólokhov still sat in the same position, only his head was thrown further back till his curly hair touched his shirt collar, and the hand holding the bottle was lifted higher and higher and trembled with the effort. The bottle was emptying perceptibly and rising still higher and his head tilting yet further back. "Why is it so long?" thought Pierre. It seemed to him that more than half an hour had elapsed. Suddenly Dólokhov made a backward movement with his spine, and his arm trembled nervously; this was sufficient to cause his whole body to slip as he sat on the sloping ledge. As he began slipping down, his head and arm wavered still more with the strain. One hand moved as if to clutch the window sill, but refrained from touching it. Pierre again covered his eyes and thought he would never open them again. Suddenly he was aware of a stir all around. He looked up: Dólokhov was standing on the window sill, with a pale but radiant face.

"It's empty."

He threw the bottle to the Englishman, who caught it neatly. Dólokhov jumped down. He smelt strongly of rum.

"Well done!... Fine fellow!... There's a bet for you!... Devil take you!" came from different sides.

The Englishman took out his purse and began counting out the money. Dólokhov stood frowning and did not speak. Pierre jumped upon the window sill.

"Gentlemen, who wishes to bet with me? I'll do the same thing!" he suddenly cried. "Even without a bet, there! Tell them to bring me a bottle. I'll do it.... Bring a bottle!"

"Let him do it, let him do it," said Dólokhov, smiling.

"What next? Have you gone mad?... No one would let you!... Why, you go giddy even on a staircase," exclaimed several voices.

"I'll drink it! Let's have a bottle of rum!" shouted Pierre, banging the table with a determined and drunken gesture and preparing to climb out of the window.

They seized him by his arms; but he was so strong that everyone who touched him was sent flying.

"No, you'll never manage him that way," said Anatole. "Wait a bit and I'll get round him.... Listen! I'll take your bet tomorrow, but now we are all going to ——'s."

"Come on then," cried Pierre. "Come on!... And we'll take Bruin with us."

And he caught the bear, took it in his arms, lifted it from the ground, and began dancing round the room with it.

CHAPTER X

Prince Vasíli kept the promise he had given to Princess Drubetskáya who had spoken to him on behalf of her only son Borís on the evening of Anna Pávlovna's soiree. The matter was mentioned to the Emperor, an exception made, and Borís transferred into the regiment of Semënov Guards with the rank of cornet. He received, however, no appointment to Kutúzov's staff despite all Anna Mikháylovna's endeavors and entreaties. Soon after Anna Pávlovna's reception Anna Mikháylovna returned to Moscow and went straight to her rich relations, the Rostóvs, with whom she stayed when in the town and where her darling Bóry, who had only just entered a regiment of the line and was being at once transferred to the Guards as a cornet, had been educated from childhood and lived for years at a time. The Guards had already left Petersburg on the tenth of August, and her son, who had remained in Moscow for his equipment, was to join them on the march to Radzivílov.

It was St. Natalia's day and the name day of two of the Rostóvs—the mother and the youngest daughter—both named Nataly. Ever since the morning, carriages with six horses had been coming and going continually, bringing visitors to the Countess Rostóva's big house on the Povarskáya, so well known to all Moscow. The countess herself and her handsome eldest daughter were in the drawing room with the visitors who came to congratulate, and who constantly succeeded one another in relays.

The countess was a woman of about forty-five, with a thin Oriental type of face, evidently worn out with childbearing—she had had twelve. A languor of motion and speech, resulting from weakness, gave her a distinguished air which inspired respect. Princess Anna MikháylovnaDrubetskáya, who as a member of the household was also seated in the drawing room, helped to receive and entertain the visitors. The young people were in one of the inner rooms, not considering it necessary to take part in receiving the visitors. The count met the guests and saw them off, inviting them all to dinner.

"I am very, very grateful to you, *moncher*," or "*ma chère*"—he called everyone without exception and without the slightest variation in his tone, "my dear," whether they were above or below him in rank—"I thank you for myself and for our two dear ones whose name day we are keeping. But mind you come to dinner or I shall be offended, *ma chère!* On behalf of the whole family I beg you to come, *moncher!*" These words he repeated to everyone without exception or variation, and with the same expression on his full, cheerful, clean-shaven face, the same firm pressure of the hand and the same quick, repeated bows. As soon as he had seen a visitor off he returned to one of those who were still in the drawing room, drew a chair toward him or her, and jauntily spreading out his legs and putting his hands on his knees with the air of a man who enjoys life and knows how to live, he swayed to and fro with dignity, offered surmises about the weather, or touched on questions of health, sometimes in Russian and sometimes in very bad but self-confident French; then again, like a man weary but unflinching in the fulfillment of duty, he rose to see some visitors off and, stroking his scanty gray hairs over his bald patch, also asked them to dinner. Sometimes on his way back from the anteroom he would pass through the conservatory and pantry into the large marble dining hall, where tables were being set out for eighty people; and looking at the footmen, who were bringing in silver and china, moving tables, and unfolding damask table linen, he would call DmítriVasílevich, a man of good family and the manager of all his affairs, and while looking with pleasure at the enormous table would say: "Well, Dmítri, you'll see that things are all as they should be? That's right! The great thing is the serving, that's it." And with a complacent sigh he would return to the drawing room.

"MáryaLvóvnaKarágina and her daughter!" announced the countess' gigantic footman in his bass voice, entering the drawing room. The countess reflected a moment and took a pinch from a gold snuffbox with her husband's portrait on it.

"I'm quite worn out by these callers. However, I'll see her and no more. She is so affected. Ask her in," she said to the footman in a sad voice, as if saying: "Very well, finish me off."

A tall, stout, and proud-looking woman, with a round-faced smiling daughter, entered the drawing room, their dresses rustling.

"Dear Countess, what an age... She has been laid up, poor child ... at the Razumóvski's ball ... and Countess Apráksina ... I was so delighted..." came the sounds of animated feminine voices, interrupting one another and mingling with the rustling of dresses and the scraping of chairs. Then one of those conversations began which last out until, at the first pause, the guests rise with a rustle of dresses and say, "I am so delighted... Mamma's health... and Countess Apráksina..." and then, again rustling, pass into the anteroom, put on cloaks or mantles, and drive away. The conversation was on the chief topic of the day: the illness of the wealthy and celebrated beau of Catherine's day, Count Bezúkhov, and about his illegitimate son Pierre, the one who had behaved so improperly at Anna Pávlovna's reception.

"I am so sorry for the poor count," said the visitor. "He is in such bad health, and now this vexation about his son is enough to kill him!"

"What is that?" asked the countess as if she did not know what the visitor alluded to, though she had already heard about the cause of Count Bezúkhov's distress some fifteen times.

"That's what comes of a modern education," exclaimed the visitor. "It seems that while he was abroad this young man was allowed to do as he liked, now in Petersburg I hear he has been doing such terrible things that he has been expelled by the police."

"You don't say so!" replied the countess.

"He chose his friends badly," interposed Anna Mikháylovna. "Prince Vasíli's son, he, and a certain Dólokhov have, it is said, been up to heaven only knows what! And they have had to suffer for it. Dólokhov has been degraded to the ranks and Bezúkhov's son sent back to Moscow. Anatole Kurágin's father managed somehow to get his son's affair hushed up, but even he was ordered out of Petersburg."

"But what have they been up to?" asked the countess.

"They are regular brigands, especially Dólokhov," replied the visitor. "He is a son of MáryaIvánovnaDólokhova, such a worthy woman, but there, just fancy! Those three got hold of a bear somewhere, put it in a carriage, and set off with it to visit some actresses! The police tried to interfere, and what did the young men do? They tied a policeman and the bear back to back and put the bear into the Moyka Canal. And there was the bear swimming about with the policeman on his back!"

"What a nice figure the policeman must have cut, my dear!" shouted the count, dying with laughter.

"Oh, how dreadful! How can you laugh at it, Count?"

Yet the ladies themselves could not help laughing.

"It was all they could do to rescue the poor man," continued the visitor. "And to think it is Cyril VladímirovichBezúkhov's son who amuses himself in this sensible manner! And he was said to be so well educated and clever. This is all that his foreign education has done for him! I hope that here in Moscow no one will receive him, in spite of his money. They wanted to introduce him to me, but I quite declined: I have my daughters to consider."

"Why do you say this young man is so rich?" asked the countess, turning away from the girls, who at once assumed an air of inattention. "His children are all illegitimate. I think Pierre also is illegitimate."

The visitor made a gesture with her hand.

"I should think he has a score of them."

Princess Anna Mikháylovna intervened in the conversation, evidently wishing to show her connections and knowledge of what went on in society.

"The fact of the matter is," said she significantly, and also in a half whisper, "everyone knows Count Cyril's reputation.... He has lost count of his children, but this Pierre was his favorite."

"How handsome the old man still was only a year ago!" remarked the countess. "I have never seen a handsomer man."

"He is very much altered now," said Anna Mikháylovna. "Well, as I was saying, Prince Vasíli is the next heir through his wife, but the count is very fond of Pierre, looked after his education, and wrote to the Emperor about him; so that in the case of his death—and he is so ill that he may die at any moment, and Dr. Lorrain has come from Petersburg—no one knows who will inherit his immense fortune, Pierre or Prince Vasíli. Forty thousand serfs and millions of rubles! I know it all very well for Prince Vasíli told me himself. Besides, Cyril Vladímirovich is my mother's second cousin. He's also my Bóry's godfather," she added, as if she attached no importance at all to the fact.

"Prince Vasíli arrived in Moscow yesterday. I hear he has come on some inspection business," remarked the visitor.

"Yes, but between ourselves," said the princess, "that is a pretext. The fact is he has come to see Count Cyril Vladímirovich, hearing how ill he is."

"But do you know, my dear, that was a capital joke," said the count; and seeing that the elder visitor was not listening, he turned to the young ladies. "I can just imagine what a funny figure that policeman cut!"

And as he waved his arms to impersonate the policeman, his portly form again shook with a deep ringing laugh, the laugh of one who always eats well and, in particular, drinks well. "So do come and dine with us!" he said.

CHAPTER XI

Silence ensued. The countess looked at her callers, smiling affably, but not concealing the fact that she would not be distressed if they now rose and took their leave. The visitor's daughter was already smoothing down her dress with an inquiring look at her mother, when suddenly from the next room were heard the footsteps of boys and girls running to the door and the noise of a chair falling over, and a girl of thirteen, hiding something in the folds of her short muslin frock, darted in and stopped short in the middle of the room. It was evident that she had not intended her flight to bring her so far. Behind her in the doorway appeared a student with a crimson coat collar, an officer of the Guards, a girl of fifteen, and a plump rosy-faced boy in a short jacket.

The count jumped up and, swaying from side to side, spread his arms wide and threw them round the little girl who had run in.

"Ah, here she is!" he exclaimed laughing. "My pet, whose name day it is. My dear pet!"

"*Ma chère*, there is a time for everything," said the countess with feigned severity. "You spoil her, Ilyá," she added, turning to her husband.

"How do you do, my dear? I wish you many happy returns of your name day," said the visitor. "What a charming child," she added, addressing the mother.

This black-eyed, wide-mouthed girl, not pretty but full of life—with childish bare shoulders which after her run heaved and shook her bodice, with black curls tossed backward, thin bare arms, little legs in lace-frilled drawers, and feet in low slippers—was just at that charming age when a girl is no longer a child, though the child is not yet a young woman. Escaping from her father she ran to hide her flushed face in the lace of her mother's mantilla—not paying the least attention to her severe remark—and began to laugh. She laughed, and in fragmentary sentences tried to explain about a doll which she produced from the folds of her frock.

"Do you see?... My doll... Mimi... You see..." was all Natásha managed to utter (to her everything seemed funny). She leaned against her mother and burst into such a loud, ringing fit of laughter that even the prim visitor could not help joining in.

"Now then, go away and take your monstrosity with you," said the mother, pushing away her daughter with pretended sternness, and turning to the visitor she added: "She is my youngest girl."

Natásha, raising her face for a moment from her mother's mantilla, glanced up at her through tears of laughter, and again hid her face.

The visitor, compelled to look on at this family scene, thought it necessary to take some part in it.

"Tell me, my dear," said she to Natásha, "is Mimi a relation of yours? A daughter, I suppose?"

Natásha did not like the visitor's tone of condescension to childish things. She did not reply, but looked at her seriously.

Meanwhile the younger generation: Borís, the officer, Anna Mikháylovna's son; Nicholas, the undergraduate, the count's eldest son; Sónya, the count's fifteen-year-old niece, and little Pétya, his youngest boy, had all settled down in the drawing room and were obviously trying to restrain within the bounds of decorum the excitement and mirth that shone in all their faces. Evidently in the back rooms, from which they had dashed out so impetuously, the conversation had been more amusing than the drawing room talk of society scandals, the weather, and Countess Apráksina. Now and then they glanced at one another, hardly able to suppress their laughter.

The two young men, the student and the officer, friends from childhood, were of the same age and both handsome fellows, though not alike. Borís was tall and fair, and his calm and handsome face had regular, delicate features. Nicholas was short with curly hair and an open expression. Dark hairs were already showing on his upper lip, and his whole face expressed impetuosity and enthusiasm. Nicholas blushed when he entered the drawing room. He evidently tried to find something to say, but failed. Borís on the contrary at once found his footing, and related quietly and humorously how he had known that doll Mimi when she was still quite a young lady, before her nose was broken; how she had aged during the five years he had known her, and how her head had cracked right across the skull. Having said this he glanced at Natásha. She turned away from him and glanced at her younger brother, who was screwing up his eyes and shaking with suppressed laughter, and unable to control herself any longer, she jumped up and rushed from the room as fast as her nimble little feet would carry her. Borís did not laugh.

"You were meaning to go out, weren't you, Mamma? Do you want the carriage?" he asked his mother with a smile.

"Yes, yes, go and tell them to get it ready," she answered, returning his smile.

Borís quietly left the room and went in search of Natásha. The plump boy ran after them angrily, as if vexed that their program had been disturbed.

CHAPTER XII

The only young people remaining in the drawing room, not counting the young lady visitor and the countess' eldest daughter (who was four years older than her sister and behaved already like a grown-up person), were Nicholas and Sónya, the niece. Sónya was a slender little brunette with a tender look in her eyes which were veiled by long lashes, thick black plaits coiling twice round her head, and a tawny tint in her complexion and especially in the color of her slender but graceful and muscular arms and neck. By the grace of her movements, by the softness and flexibility of her small limbs, and by a certain coyness and reserve of manner, she reminded one of a pretty, half-grown kitten which promises to become a beautiful little cat. She evidently considered it proper to show an interest in the general conversation by smiling, but in spite of herself her eyes under their thick long lashes watched her cousin who was going to join the army, with such passionate girlish adoration that her smile could not for a single instant impose upon anyone, and it was clear that the kitten had settled down only to spring up with more energy and again play with her cousin as soon as they too could, like Natásha and Borís, escape from the drawing room.

"Ah yes, my dear," said the count, addressing the visitor and pointing to Nicholas, "his friend Borís has become an officer, and so for friendship's sake he is leaving the university and me, his old father, and entering the military service, my dear. And there was a place and everything waiting for him in the Archives Department! Isn't that friendship?" remarked the count in an inquiring tone.

"But they say that war has been declared," replied the visitor.

"They've been saying so a long while," said the count, "and they'll say so again and again, and that will be the end of it. My dear, there's friendship for you," he repeated. "He's joining the hussars."

The visitor, not knowing what to say, shook her head.

"It's not at all from friendship," declared Nicholas, flaring up and turning away as if from a shameful aspersion. "It is not from friendship at all; I simply feel that the army is my vocation."

He glanced at his cousin and the young lady visitor; and they were both regarding him with a smile of approbation.

"Schubert, the colonel of the Pávlograd Hussars, is dining with us today. He has been here on leave and is taking Nicholas back with him. It can't be helped!" said the count, shrugging his shoulders and speaking playfully of a matter that evidently distressed him.

"I have already told you, Papa," said his son, "that if you don't wish to let me go, I'll stay. But I know I am no use anywhere except in the army; I am not a diplomat or a government clerk.—I don't know how to hide what I feel." As he spoke he kept glancing with the flirtatiousness of a handsome youth at Sónya and the young lady visitor.

The little kitten, feasting her eyes on him, seemed ready at any moment to start her gambols again and display her kittenish nature.

"All right, all right!" said the old count. "He always flares up! This Buonaparte has turned all their heads; they all think of how he rose from an ensign and became Emperor. Well, well, God grant it," he added, not noticing his visitor's sarcastic smile.

The elders began talking about Bonaparte. Julie Karágina turned to young Rostóv.

"What a pity you weren't at the Arkhárovs' on Thursday. It was so dull without you," said she, giving him a tender smile.

The young man, flattered, sat down nearer to her with a coquettish smile, and engaged the smiling Julie in a confidential conversation without at all noticing that his involuntary smile had stabbed the heart of Sónya, who blushed and smiled unnaturally. In the midst of his talk he glanced round at her. She gave him a passionately angry glance, and hardly able to restrain her tears and maintain the artificial smile on her lips, she got up and left the room. All Nicholas' animation vanished. He waited for the first pause in the conversation, and then with a distressed face left the room to find Sónya.

"How plainly all these young people wear their hearts on their sleeves!" said Anna Mikháylovna, pointing to Nicholas as he went out. "Cousinage—dangereuxvoisinage,"* she added.

* Cousinhood is a dangerous neighborhood.

"Yes," said the countess when the brightness these young people had brought into the room had vanished; and as if answering a question no one had put but which was always in her mind, "and how much suffering, how much anxiety one has had to go through that we might rejoice in them now! And yet really the anxiety is greater now than the joy. One is always, always anxious! Especially just at this age, so dangerous both for girls and boys."

"It all depends on the bringing up," remarked the visitor.

"Yes, you're quite right," continued the countess. "Till now I have always, thank God, been my children's friend and had their full confidence," said she, repeating the mistake of so many parents who imagine that their children have no secrets from them. "I know I shall always be my daughters' first confidante, and that if Nicholas, with his impulsive nature, does get into mischief (a boy can't help it), he will all the same never be like those Petersburg young men."

"Yes, they are splendid, splendid youngsters," chimed in the count, who always solved questions that seemed to him perplexing by deciding that everything was splendid. "Just fancy: wants to be an hussar. What's one to do, my dear?"

"What a charming creature your younger girl is," said the visitor; "a little volcano!"

"Yes, a regular volcano," said the count. "Takes after me! And what a voice she has; though she's my daughter, I tell the truth when I say she'll be a singer, a second Salomoni! We have engaged an Italian to give her lessons."

"Isn't she too young? I have heard that it harms the voice to train it at that age."

"Oh no, not at all too young!" replied the count. "Why, our mothers used to be married at twelve or thirteen."

"And she's in love with Borís already. Just fancy!" said the countess with a gentle smile, looking at Borís and went on, evidently concerned with a thought that always occupied her: "Now you see if I were to be severe with her and to forbid it ... goodness knows what they might be up to on the sly" (she meant that they would be kissing), "but as it is, I know every word she utters. She will come running to me of her own accord in the evening and tell me everything. Perhaps I spoil her, but really that seems the best plan. With her elder sister I was stricter."

"Yes, I was brought up quite differently," remarked the handsome elder daughter, Countess Véra, with a smile.

But the smile did not enhance Véra's beauty as smiles generally do; on the contrary it gave her an unnatural, and therefore unpleasant, expression. Véra was good-looking, not at all stupid, quick at learning, was well brought up, and had a pleasant voice; what she said was true and appropriate, yet, strange to say, everyone—the visitors and countess alike—turned to look at her as if wondering why she had said it, and they all felt awkward.

"People are always too clever with their eldest children and try to make something exceptional of them," said the visitor.

"What's the good of denying it, my dear? Our dear countess was too clever with Véra," said the count. "Well, what of that? She's turned out splendidly all the same," he added, winking at Véra.

The guests got up and took their leave, promising to return to dinner.

"What manners! I thought they would never go," said the countess, when she had seen her guests out.

CHAPTER XIII

When Natásha ran out of the drawing room she only went as far as the conservatory. There she paused and stood listening to the conversation in the drawing room, waiting for Borís to come out. She was already growing impatient, and stamped her foot, ready to cry at his not coming at once, when she heard the young man's discreet steps approaching neither quickly nor slowly. At this Natásha dashed swiftly among the flower tubs and hid there.

Borís paused in the middle of the room, looked round, brushed a little dust from the sleeve of his uniform, and going up to a mirror examined his handsome face. Natásha, very still, peered out from her ambush, waiting to see what he would do. He stood a little while before the glass, smiled, and walked toward the other door. Natásha was about to call him but changed her mind. "Let him look for me," thought she. Hardly had Borís gone than Sónya, flushed, in tears, and muttering angrily, came in at the other door. Natásha checked her first impulse to run out to her, and remained in her hiding place, watching—as under an invisible cap—to see what went on in the world. She was experiencing a new and peculiar pleasure. Sónya, muttering to herself, kept looking round toward the drawing room door. It opened and Nicholas came in.

"Sónya, what is the matter with you? How can you?" said he, running up to her.

"It's nothing, nothing; leave me alone!" sobbed Sónya.

"Ah, I know what it is."

"Well, if you do, so much the better, and you can go back to her!"

"Só-o-onya! Look here! How can you torture me and yourself like that, for a mere fancy?" said Nicholas taking her hand.

Sónya did not pull it away, and left off crying. Natásha, not stirring and scarcely breathing, watched from her ambush with sparkling eyes. "What will happen now?" thought she.

"Sónya! What is anyone in the world to me? You alone are everything!" said Nicholas. "And I will prove it to you."

"I don't like you to talk like that."

"Well, then, I won't; only forgive me, Sónya!" He drew her to him and kissed her.

"Oh, how nice," thought Natásha; and when Sónya and Nicholas had gone out of the conservatory she followed and called Borís to her.

"Borís, come here," said she with a sly and significant look. "I have something to tell you. Here, here!" and she led him into the conservatory to the place among the tubs where she had been hiding.

Borís followed her, smiling.

"What is the *something?*" asked he.

She grew confused, glanced round, and, seeing the doll she had thrown down on one of the tubs, picked it up.

"Kiss the doll," said she.

Borís looked attentively and kindly at her eager face, but did not reply.

"Don't you want to? Well, then, come here," said she, and went further in among the plants and threw down the doll. "Closer, closer!" she whispered.

She caught the young officer by his cuffs, and a look of solemnity and fear appeared on her flushed face.

"And me? Would you like to kiss me?" she whispered almost inaudibly, glancing up at him from under her brows, smiling, and almost crying from excitement.

Borís blushed.

"How funny you are!" he said, bending down to her and blushing still more, but he waited and did nothing.

Suddenly she jumped up onto a tub to be higher than he, embraced him so that both her slender bare arms clasped him above his neck, and, tossing back her hair, kissed him full on the lips. Then she slipped down among the flowerpots on the other side of the tubs and stood, hanging her head.

"Natásha," he said, "you know that I love you, but...."

"You are in love with me?" Natásha broke in.

"Yes, I am, but please don't let us do like that.... In another four years ... then I will ask for your hand."

Natásha considered.

"Thirteen, fourteen, fifteen, sixteen," she counted on her slender little fingers. "All right! Then it's settled?"

A smile of joy and satisfaction lit up her eager face.

"Settled!" replied Borís.

"Forever?" said the little girl. "Till death itself?"

She took his arm and with a happy face went with him into the adjoining sitting room.

CHAPTER XIV

After receiving her visitors, the countess was so tired that she gave orders to admit no more, but the porter was told to be sure to invite to dinner all who came "to congratulate." The countess wished to have a tête-à-tête talk with the friend of her childhood, Princess Anna Mikháylovna, whom she had not seen properly since she returned from Petersburg. Anna Mikháylovna, with her tear-worn but pleasant face, drew her chair nearer to that of the countess.

"With you I will be quite frank," said Anna Mikháylovna. "There are not many left of us old friends! That's why I so value your friendship."

Anna Mikháylovna looked at Véra and paused. The countess pressed her friend's hand.

"Véra," she said to her eldest daughter who was evidently not a favorite, "how is it you have so little tact? Don't you see you are not wanted here? Go to the other girls, or..."

The handsome Véra smiled contemptuously but did not seem at all hurt.

"If you had told me sooner, Mamma, I would have gone," she replied as she rose to go to her own room.

But as she passed the sitting room she noticed two couples sitting, one pair at each window. She stopped and smiled scornfully. Sónya was sitting close to Nicholas who was copying out some verses for her, the first he had ever written. Borís and Natásha were at the other window and ceased talking when Véra entered. Sónya and Natásha looked at Véra with guilty, happy faces.

It was pleasant and touching to see these little girls in love; but apparently the sight of them roused no pleasant feeling in Véra.

"How often have I asked you not to take my things?" she said. "You have a room of your own," and she took the inkstand from Nicholas.

"In a minute, in a minute," he said, dipping his pen.

"You always manage to do things at the wrong time," continued Véra. "You came rushing into the drawing room so that everyone felt ashamed of you."

Though what she said was quite just, perhaps for that very reason no one replied, and the four simply looked at one another. She lingered in the room with the inkstand in her hand.

"And at your age what secrets can there be between Natásha and Borís, or between you two? It's all nonsense!"

"Now, Véra, what does it matter to you?" said Natásha in defense, speaking very gently.

She seemed that day to be more than ever kind and affectionate to everyone.

"Very silly," said Véra. "I am ashamed of you. Secrets indeed!"

"All have secrets of their own," answered Natásha, getting warmer. "We don't interfere with you and Berg."

"I should think not," said Véra, "because there can never be anything wrong in my behavior. But I'll just tell Mamma how you are behaving with Borís."

"Natályallyníchna behaves very well to me," remarked Borís. "I have nothing to complain of."

"Don't, Borís! You are such a diplomat that it is really tiresome," said Natásha in a mortified voice that trembled slightly. (She used the word "diplomat," which was just then much in vogue among the children, in the special sense they attached to it.) "Why does she bother me?" And she added, turning to Véra, "You'll never understand it, because you've never loved anyone. You have no heart! You are a Madame de Genlis and nothing more" (this nickname, bestowed on

Véra by Nicholas, was considered very stinging), "and your greatest pleasure is to be unpleasant to people! Go and flirt with Berg as much as you please," she finished quickly.

"I shall at any rate not run after a young man before visitors..."

"Well, now you've done what you wanted," put in Nicholas—"said unpleasant things to everyone and upset them. Let's go to the nursery."

All four, like a flock of scared birds, got up and left the room.

"The unpleasant things were said to me," remarked Véra, "I said none to anyone."

"Madame de Genlis! Madame de Genlis!" shouted laughing voices through the door.

The handsome Véra, who produced such an irritating and unpleasant effect on everyone, smiled and, evidently unmoved by what had been said to her, went to the looking glass and arranged her hair and scarf. Looking at her own handsome face she seemed to become still colder and calmer.

In the drawing room the conversation was still going on.

"Ah, my dear," said the countess, "my life is not all roses either. Don't I know that at the rate we are living our means won't last long? It's all the Club and his easygoing nature. Even in the country do we get any rest? Theatricals, hunting, and heaven knows what besides! But don't let's talk about me; tell me how you managed everything. I often wonder at you, Annette—how at your age you can rush off alone in a carriage to Moscow, to Petersburg, to those ministers and great people, and know how to deal with them all! It's quite astonishing. How did you get things settled? I couldn't possibly do it."

"Ah, my love," answered Anna Mikháylovna, "God grant you never know what it is to be left a widow without means and with a son you love to distraction! One learns many things then," she added with a certain pride. "That lawsuit taught me much. When I want to see one of those big people I write a note: 'Princess So-and-So desires an interview with So and-So,' and then I take a cab and go myself two, three, or four times—till I get what I want. I don't mind what they think of me."

"Well, and to whom did you apply about Bóry?" asked the countess. "You see yours is already an officer in the Guards, while my Nicholas is going as a cadet. There's no one to interest himself for him. To whom did you apply?"

"To Prince Vasíli. He was so kind. He at once agreed to everything, and put the matter before the Emperor," said Princess Anna Mikháylovna enthusiastically, quite forgetting all the humiliation she had endured to gain her end.

"Has Prince Vasíli aged much?" asked the countess. "I have not seen him since we acted together at the Rumyántsovs' theatricals. I expect he has forgotten me. He paid me attentions in those days," said the countess, with a smile.

"He is just the same as ever," replied Anna Mikháylovna, "overflowing with amiability. His position has not turned his head at all. He said to me, 'I am sorry I can do so little for you, dear Princess. I am at your command.' Yes, he is a fine fellow and a very kind relation. But, Nataly, you know my love for my son: I would do anything for his happiness! And my affairs are in such a bad way that my position is now a terrible one," continued Anna Mikháylovna, sadly, dropping her voice. "My wretched lawsuit takes all I have and makes no progress. Would you believe it, I have literally not a penny and don't know how to equip Borís." She took out her handkerchief and began to cry. "I need five hundred rubles, and have only one twenty-five-ruble note. I am in such a state.... My only hope now is in Count Cyril VladímirovichBezúkhov. If he will not assist his godson—you know he is Bóry's godfather—and allow him something for his maintenance, all my trouble will have been thrown away.... I shall not be able to equip him."

The countess' eyes filled with tears and she pondered in silence.

"I often think, though, perhaps it's a sin," said the princess, "that here lives Count Cyril VladímirovichBezúkhov so rich, all alone... that tremendous fortune... and what is his life worth? It's a burden to him, and Bóry's life is only just beginning...."

"Surely he will leave something to Borís," said the countess.

"Heaven only knows, my dear! These rich grandees are so selfish. Still, I will take Borís and go to see him at once, and I shall speak to him straight out. Let people think what they will of me, it's really all the same to me when my son's fate is at stake." The princess rose. "It's now two o'clock and you dine at four. There will just be time."

And like a practical Petersburg lady who knows how to make the most of time, Anna Mikháylovna sent someone to call her son, and went into the anteroom with him.

"Good-by, my dear," said she to the countess who saw her to the door, and added in a whisper so that her son should not hear, "Wish me good luck."

"Are you going to Count Cyril Vladímirovich, my dear?" said the count coming out from the dining hall into the anteroom, and he added: "If he is better, ask Pierre to dine with us. He has been to the house, you know, and danced with the children. Be sure to invite him, my dear. We will see how Tarás distinguishes himself today. He says Count Orlóv never gave such a dinner as ours will be!"

CHAPTER XV

"My dear Borís," said Princess Anna Mikháylovna to her son as Countess Rostóva's carriage in which they were seated drove over the straw covered street and turned into the wide courtyard of Count Cyril VladímirovichBezúkhov's house. "My dear Borís," said the mother, drawing her hand from beneath her old mantle and laying it timidly and tenderly on her son's arm, "be affectionate and attentive to him. Count Cyril Vladímirovich is your godfather after all, and your future depends on him. Remember that, my dear, and be nice to him, as you so well know how to be."

"If only I knew that anything besides humiliation would come of it..." answered her son coldly. "But I have promised and will do it for your sake."

Although the hall porter saw someone's carriage standing at the entrance, after scrutinizing the mother and son (who without asking to be announced had passed straight through the glass porch between the rows of statues in niches) and looking significantly at the lady's old cloak, he asked whether they wanted the count or the princesses, and, hearing that they wished to see the count, said his excellency was worse today, and that his excellency was not receiving anyone.

"We may as well go back," said the son in French.

"My dear!" exclaimed his mother imploringly, again laying her hand on his arm as if that touch might soothe or rouse him.

Borís said no more, but looked inquiringly at his mother without taking off his cloak.

"My friend," said Anna Mikháylovna in gentle tones, addressing the hall porter, "I know Count Cyril Vladímirovich is very ill... that's why I have come... I am a relation. I shall not disturb him, my friend... I only need see Prince VasíliSergéevich: he is staying here, is he not? Please announce me."

The hall porter sullenly pulled a bell that rang upstairs, and turned away.

"Princess Drubetskáya to see Prince VasíliSergéevich," he called to a footman dressed in knee breeches, shoes, and a swallow-tail coat, who ran downstairs and looked over from the halfway landing.

The mother smoothed the folds of her dyed silk dress before a large Venetian mirror in the wall, and in her trodden-down shoes briskly ascended the carpeted stairs.

"My dear," she said to her son, once more stimulating him by a touch, "you promised me!"

The son, lowering his eyes, followed her quietly.

They entered the large hall, from which one of the doors led to the apartments assigned to Prince Vasíli.

Just as the mother and son, having reached the middle of the hall, were about to ask their way of an elderly footman who had sprung up as they entered, the bronze handle of one of the doors turned and Prince Vasíli came out—wearing a velvet coat with a single star on his breast, as was his custom when at home—taking leave of a good-looking, dark-haired man. This was the celebrated Petersburg doctor, Lorrain.

"Then it is certain?" said the prince.

"Prince, *humanum esterrare*, * but..." replied the doctor, swallowing his *r*'s, and pronouncing the Latin words with a French accent.

* To err is human.

"Very well, very well..."

Seeing Anna Mikháylovna and her son, Prince Vasíli dismissed the doctor with a bow and approached them silently and with a look of inquiry. The son noticed that an expression of profound sorrow suddenly clouded his mother's face, and he smiled slightly.

"Ah, Prince! In what sad circumstances we meet again! And how is our dear invalid?" said she, as though unaware of the cold offensive look fixed on her.

Prince Vasíli stared at her and at Borís questioningly and perplexed. Borís bowed politely. Prince Vasíli without acknowledging the bow turned to Anna Mikháylovna, answering her query by a movement of the head and lips indicating very little hope for the patient.

"Is it possible?" exclaimed Anna Mikháylovna. "Oh, how awful! It is terrible to think.... This is my son," she added, indicating Borís. "He wanted to thank you himself."

Borís bowed again politely.

"Believe me, Prince, a mother's heart will never forget what you have done for us."

"I am glad I was able to do you a service, my dear Anna Mikháylovna," said Prince Vasíli, arranging his lace frill, and in tone and manner, here in Moscow to Anna Mikháylovna whom he had placed under an obligation, assuming an air of much greater importance than he had done in Petersburg at Anna Schérer's reception.

"Try to serve well and show yourself worthy," added he, addressing Borís with severity. "I am glad.... Are you here on leave?" he went on in his usual tone of indifference.

"I am awaiting orders to join my new regiment, your excellency," replied Borís, betraying neither annoyance at the prince's brusque manner nor a desire to enter into conversation, but speaking so quietly and respectfully that the prince gave him a searching glance.

"Are you living with your mother?"

"I am living at Countess Rostóva's," replied Borís, again adding, "your excellency."

"That is, with IlyáRostóv who married Nataly Shinshiná," said Anna Mikháylovna.

"I know, I know," answered Prince Vasíli in his monotonous voice. "I never could understand how Nataly made up her mind to marry that unlicked bear! A perfectly absurd and stupid fellow, and a gambler too, I am told."

"But a very kind man, Prince," said Anna Mikháylovna with a pathetic smile, as though she too knew that Count Rostóv deserved this censure, but asked him not to be too hard on the poor old man.

War and Peace

"What do the doctors say?" asked the princess after a pause, her worn face again expressing deep sorrow.

"They give little hope," replied the prince.

"And I should so like to thank *Uncle* once for all his kindness to me and Borís. He is his godson," she added, her tone suggesting that this fact ought to give Prince Vasíli much satisfaction.

Prince Vasíli became thoughtful and frowned. Anna Mikháylovna saw that he was afraid of finding in her a rival for Count Bezúkhov's fortune, and hastened to reassure him.

"If it were not for my sincere affection and devotion to *Uncle*," said she, uttering the word with peculiar assurance and unconcern, "I know his character: noble, upright ... but you see he has no one with him except the young princesses.... They are still young...." She bent her head and continued in a whisper: "Has he performed his final duty, Prince? How priceless are those last moments! It can make things no worse, and it is absolutely necessary to prepare him if he is so ill. We women, Prince," and she smiled tenderly, "always know how to say these things. I absolutely must see him, however painful it may be for me. I am used to suffering."

Evidently the prince understood her, and also understood, as he had done at Anna Pávlovna's, that it would be difficult to get rid of Anna Mikháylovna.

"Would not such a meeting be too trying for him, dear Anna Mikháylovna?" said he. "Let us wait until evening. The doctors are expecting a crisis."

"But one cannot delay, Prince, at such a moment! Consider that the welfare of his soul is at stake. Ah, it is awful: the duties of a Christian..."

A door of one of the inner rooms opened and one of the princesses, the count's niece, entered with a cold, stern face. The length of her body was strikingly out of proportion to her short legs. Prince Vasíli turned to her.

"Well, how is he?"

"Still the same; but what can you expect, this noise..." said the princess, looking at Anna Mikháylovna as at a stranger.

"Ah, my dear, I hardly knew you," said Anna Mikháylovna with a happy smile, ambling lightly up to the count's niece. "I have come, and am at your service to help you nurse *my uncle*. I imagine what you have gone through," and she sympathetically turned up her eyes.

The princess gave no reply and did not even smile, but left the room as Anna Mikháylovna took off her gloves and, occupying the position she had conquered, settled down in an armchair, inviting Prince Vasíli to take a seat beside her.

"Borís," she said to her son with a smile, "I shall go in to see the count, my uncle; but you, my dear, had better go to Pierre meanwhile and don't forget to give him the Rostóvs' invitation. They ask him to dinner. I suppose he won't go?" she continued, turning to the prince.

"On the contrary," replied the prince, who had plainly become depressed, "I shall be only too glad if you relieve me of that young man.... Here he is, and the count has not once asked for him."

He shrugged his shoulders. A footman conducted Borís down one flight of stairs and up another, to Pierre's rooms.

CHAPTER XVI

Pierre, after all, had not managed to choose a career for himself in Petersburg, and had been expelled from there for riotous conduct and sent to Moscow. The story told about him at Count Rostóv's was true. Pierre had taken part in tying a policeman to a bear. He had now been for some days in Moscow and was staying as usual at his father's house. Though he expected that the story of his escapade would be already known in Moscow and that the ladies about his father—who were never favorably disposed toward him—would have used it to turn the count against him, he nevertheless on the day of his arrival went to his father's part of the house. Entering the drawing room, where the princesses spent most of their time, he greeted the ladies, two of whom were sitting at embroidery frames while a third read aloud. It was the eldest who was reading—the one who had met Anna Mikháylovna. The two younger ones were embroidering: both were rosy and pretty and they differed only in that one had a little mole on her lip which made her much prettier. Pierre was received as if he were a corpse or a leper. The eldest princess paused in her reading and silently stared at him with frightened eyes; the second assumed precisely the same expression; while the youngest, the one with the mole, who was of a cheerful and lively disposition, bent over her frame to hide a smile probably evoked by the amusing scene she foresaw. She drew her wool down through the canvas and, scarcely able to refrain from laughing, stooped as if trying to make out the pattern.

"How do you do, cousin?" said Pierre. "You don't recognize me?"

"I recognize you only too well, too well."

"How is the count? Can I see him?" asked Pierre, awkwardly as usual, but unabashed.

"The count is suffering physically and mentally, and apparently you have done your best to increase his mental sufferings."

"Can I see the count?" Pierre again asked.

"Hm.... If you wish to kill him, to kill him outright, you can see him... Olga, go and see whether Uncle's beef tea is ready—it is almost time," she added, giving Pierre to understand that they were busy, and busy making his father comfortable, while evidently he, Pierre, was only busy causing him annoyance.

Olga went out. Pierre stood looking at the sisters; then he bowed and said: "Then I will go to my rooms. You will let me know when I can see him."

And he left the room, followed by the low but ringing laughter of the sister with the mole.

Next day Prince Vasíli had arrived and settled in the count's house. He sent for Pierre and said to him: "My dear fellow, if you are going to behave here as you did in Petersburg, you will end very badly; that is all I have to say to you. The count is very, very ill, and you must not see him at all."

Since then Pierre had not been disturbed and had spent the whole time in his rooms upstairs.

When Borís appeared at his door Pierre was pacing up and down his room, stopping occasionally at a corner to make menacing gestures at the wall, as if running a sword through an invisible foe, and glaring savagely over his spectacles, and then again resuming his walk, muttering indistinct words, shrugging his shoulders and gesticulating.

"England is done for," said he, scowling and pointing his finger at someone unseen. "Mr. Pitt, as a traitor to the nation and to the rights of man, is sentenced to..." But before Pierre—who at that moment imagined himself to be Napoleon in person and to have just effected the dangerous crossing of the Straits of Dover and captured London—could pronounce Pitt's sentence, he saw a well-built and handsome young officer entering his room. Pierre paused. He had left Moscow when Borís was a boy of fourteen, and had quite forgotten him, but in his usual impulsive and hearty way he took Borís by the hand with a friendly smile.

"Do you remember me?" asked Borís quietly with a pleasant smile. "I have come with my mother to see the count, but it seems he is not well."

"Yes, it seems he is ill. People are always disturbing him," answered Pierre, trying to remember who this young man was.

Borís felt that Pierre did not recognize him but did not consider it necessary to introduce himself, and without experiencing the least embarrassment looked Pierre straight in the face.

"Count Rostóv asks you to come to dinner today," said he, after a considerable pause which made Pierre feel uncomfortable.

"Ah, Count Rostóv!" exclaimed Pierre joyfully. "Then you are his son, Ilyá? Only fancy, I didn't know you at first. Do you remember how we went to the Sparrow Hills with Madame Jacquot?... It's such an age..."

"You are mistaken," said Borís deliberately, with a bold and slightly sarcastic smile. "I am Borís, son of Princess Anna MikháylovnaDrubetskáya. Rostóv, the father, is Ilyá, and his son is Nicholas. I never knew any Madame Jacquot."

Pierre shook his head and arms as if attacked by mosquitoes or bees.

"Oh dear, what am I thinking about? I've mixed everything up. One has so many relatives in Moscow! So you are Borís? Of course. Well, now we know where we are. And what do you think of the Boulogne expedition? The English will come off badly, you know, if Napoleon gets across the Channel. I think the expedition is quite feasible. If only Villeneuve doesn't make a mess of things!"

Borís knew nothing about the Boulogne expedition; he did not read the papers and it was the first time he had heard Villeneuve's name.

"We here in Moscow are more occupied with dinner parties and scandal than with politics," said he in his quiet ironical tone. "I know nothing about it and have not thought about it. Moscow is chiefly busy with gossip," he continued. "Just now they are talking about you and your father."

Pierre smiled in his good-natured way as if afraid for his companion's sake that the latter might say something he would afterwards regret. But Borís spoke distinctly, clearly, and dryly, looking straight into Pierre's eyes.

"Moscow has nothing else to do but gossip," Borís went on. "Everybody is wondering to whom the count will leave his fortune, though he may perhaps outlive us all, as I sincerely hope he will..."

"Yes, it is all very horrid," interrupted Pierre, "very horrid."

Pierre was still afraid that this officer might inadvertently say something disconcerting to himself.

"And it must seem to you," said Borís flushing slightly, but not changing his tone or attitude, "it must seem to you that everyone is trying to get something out of the rich man?"

"So it does," thought Pierre.

"But I just wish to say, to avoid misunderstandings, that you are quite mistaken if you reckon me or my mother among such people. We are very poor, but for my own part at any rate, for the very reason that your father is rich, I don't regard myself as a relation of his, and neither I nor my mother would ever ask or take anything from him."

For a long time Pierre could not understand, but when he did, he jumped up from the sofa, seized Borís under the elbow in his quick, clumsy way, and, blushing far more than Borís, began to speak with a feeling of mingled shame and vexation.

"Well, this is strange! Do you suppose I... who could think?... I know very well..."

But Borís again interrupted him.

"I am glad I have spoken out fully. Perhaps you did not like it? You must excuse me," said he, putting Pierre at ease instead of being put at ease by him, "but I hope I have not offended you. I always make it a rule to speak out... Well, what answer am I to take? Will you come to dinner at the Rostóvs'?"

And Borís, having apparently relieved himself of an onerous duty and extricated himself from an awkward situation and placed another in it, became quite pleasant again.

"No, but I say," said Pierre, calming down, "you are a wonderful fellow! What you have just said is good, very good. Of course you don't know me. We have not met for such a long time... not since we were children. You might think that I... I understand, quite understand. I could not have done it myself, I should not have had the courage, but it's splendid. I am very glad to have made your acquaintance. It's queer," he added after a pause, "that you should have suspected me!" He began to laugh. "Well, what of it! I hope we'll get better acquainted," and he pressed Borís' hand. "Do you know, I have not once been in to see the count. He has not sent for me.... I am sorry for him as a man, but what can one do?"

"And so you think Napoleon will manage to get an army across?" asked Borís with a smile.

Pierre saw that Borís wished to change the subject, and being of the same mind he began explaining the advantages and disadvantages of the Boulogne expedition.

A footman came in to summon Borís—the princess was going. Pierre, in order to make Borís' better acquaintance, promised to come to dinner, and warmly pressing his hand looked affectionately over his spectacles into Borís' eyes. After he had gone Pierre continued pacing up and down the room for a long time, no longer piercing an imaginary foe with his imaginary sword, but smiling at the remembrance of that pleasant, intelligent, and resolute young man.

As often happens in early youth, especially to one who leads a lonely life, he felt an unaccountable tenderness for this young man and made up his mind that they would be friends.

Prince Vasíli saw the princess off. She held a handkerchief to her eyes and her face was tearful.

"It is dreadful, dreadful!" she was saying, "but cost me what it may I shall do my duty. I will come and spend the night. He must not be left like this. Every moment is precious. I can't think why his nieces put it off. Perhaps God will help me to find a way to prepare him!... Adieu, Prince! May God support you..."

"*Adieu, ma bonne,*" answered Prince Vasíli turning away from her.

"Oh, he is in a dreadful state," said the mother to her son when they were in the carriage. "He hardly recognizes anybody."

"I don't understand, Mamma—what is his attitude to Pierre?" asked the son.

"The will will show that, my dear; our fate also depends on it."

"But why do you expect that he will leave us anything?"

"Ah, my dear! He is so rich, and we are so poor!"

"Well, that is hardly a sufficient reason, Mamma..."

"Oh, Heaven! How ill he is!" exclaimed the mother.

CHAPTER XVII

After Anna Mikháylovna had driven off with her son to visit Count Cyril VladímirovichBezúkhov, Countess Rostóva sat for a long time all alone applying her handkerchief to her eyes. At last she rang.

"What is the matter with you, my dear?" she said crossly to the maid who kept her waiting some minutes. "Don't you wish to serve me? Then I'll find you another place."

The countess was upset by her friend's sorrow and humiliating poverty, and was therefore out of sorts, a state of mind which with her always found expression in calling her maid "my dear" and speaking to her with exaggerated politeness.

"I am very sorry, ma'am," answered the maid.

"Ask the count to come to me."

The count came waddling in to see his wife with a rather guilty look as usual.

"Well, little countess? What a *sauté* of game *au madère* we are to have, my dear! I tasted it. The thousand rubles I paid for Tarás were not ill-spent. He is worth it!"

He sat down by his wife, his elbows on his knees and his hands ruffling his gray hair.

"What are your commands, little countess?"

"You see, my dear... What's that mess?" she said, pointing to his waistcoat. "It's the *sauté*, most likely," she added with a smile. "Well, you see, Count, I want some money."

Her face became sad.

"Oh, little countess!" ... and the count began bustling to get out his pocketbook.

"I want a great deal, Count! I want five hundred rubles," and taking out her cambric handkerchief she began wiping her husband's waistcoat.

"Yes, immediately, immediately! Hey, who's there?" he called out in a tone only used by persons who are certain that those they call will rush to obey the summons. "Send Dmítri to me!"

Dmítri, a man of good family who had been brought up in the count's house and now managed all his affairs, stepped softly into the room.

"This is what I want, my dear fellow," said the count to the deferential young man who had entered. "Bring me..." he reflected a moment, "yes, bring me seven hundred rubles, yes! But mind, don't bring me such tattered and dirty notes as last time, but nice clean ones for the countess."

"Yes, Dmítri, clean ones, please," said the countess, sighing deeply.

"When would you like them, your excellency?" asked Dmítri. "Allow me to inform you... But, don't be uneasy," he added, noticing that the count was beginning to breathe heavily and quickly which was always a sign of approaching anger. "I was forgetting... Do you wish it brought at once?"

"Yes, yes; just so! Bring it. Give it to the countess."

"What a treasure that Dmítri is," added the count with a smile when the young man had departed. "There is never any 'impossible' with him. That's a thing I hate! Everything is possible."

"Ah, money, Count, money! How much sorrow it causes in the world," said the countess. "But I am in great need of this sum."

"You, my little countess, are a notorious spendthrift," said the count, and having kissed his wife's hand he went back to his study.

When Anna Mikháylovna returned from Count Bezúkhov's the money, all in clean notes, was lying ready under a handkerchief on the countess' little table, and Anna Mikháylovna noticed that something was agitating her.

"Well, my dear?" asked the countess.

"Oh, what a terrible state he is in! One would not know him, he is so ill! I was only there a few moments and hardly said a word..."

"Annette, for heaven's sake don't refuse me," the countess began, with a blush that looked very strange on her thin, dignified, elderly face, and she took the money from under the handkerchief.

Anna Mikháylovna instantly guessed her intention and stooped to be ready to embrace the countess at the appropriate moment.

"This is for Borís from me, for his outfit."

Anna Mikháylovna was already embracing her and weeping. The countess wept too. They wept because they were friends, and because they were kindhearted, and because they—friends from childhood—had to think about such a base thing as money, and because their youth was over.... But those tears were pleasant to them both.

CHAPTER XVIII

Countess Rostóva, with her daughters and a large number of guests, was already seated in the drawing room. The count took the gentlemen into his study and showed them his choice collection of Turkish pipes. From time to time he went out to ask: "Hasn't she come yet?" They were expecting MáryaDmítrievnaAkhrosímova, known in society as *le terrible dragon*, a lady distinguished not for wealth or rank, but for common sense and frank plainness of speech. MáryaDmítrievna was known to the Imperial family as well as to all Moscow and Petersburg, and both cities wondered at her, laughed privately at her rudenesses, and told good stories about her, while none the less all without exception respected and feared her.

In the count's room, which was full of tobacco smoke, they talked of the war that had been announced in a manifesto, and about the recruiting. None of them had yet seen the manifesto, but they all knew it had appeared. The count sat on the sofa between two guests who were smoking and talking. He neither smoked nor talked, but bending his head first to one side and then to the other watched the smokers with evident pleasure and listened to the conversation of his two neighbors, whom he egged on against each other.

One of them was a sallow, clean-shaven civilian with a thin and wrinkled face, already growing old, though he was dressed like a most fashionable young man. He sat with his legs up on the sofa as if quite at home and, having stuck an amber mouthpiece far into his mouth, was inhaling the smoke spasmodically and screwing up his eyes. This was an old bachelor, Shinshín, a cousin of the countess', a man with "a sharp tongue" as they said in Moscow society. He seemed to be condescending to his companion. The latter, a fresh, rosy officer of the Guards, irreproachably washed, brushed, and buttoned, held his pipe in the middle of his mouth and with red lips gently inhaled the smoke, letting it escape from his handsome mouth in rings. This was Lieutenant Berg, an officer in the Semënov regiment with whom Borís was to travel to join the army, and about whom Natásha had teased her elder sister Véra, speaking of Berg as her "intended." The count sat between them and listened attentively. His favorite occupation when not playing boston, a card game he was very fond of, was that of listener, especially when he succeeded in setting two loquacious talkers at one another.

"Well, then, old chap, *montrèshonorable* Alphonse Kárlovich," said Shinshín, laughing ironically and mixing the most ordinary Russian expressions with the choicest French phrases—which was a peculiarity of his speech. "*Vouscomptezvous faire des rentes sur l'état*; * you want to make something out of your company?"

* You expect to make an income out of the government.

"No, Peter Nikoláevich; I only want to show that in the cavalry the advantages are far less than in the infantry. Just consider my own position now, Peter Nikoláevich..."

Berg always spoke quietly, politely, and with great precision. His conversation always related entirely to himself; he would remain calm and silent when the talk related to any topic that had no direct bearing on himself. He could remain silent for hours without being at all put out of countenance himself or making others uncomfortable, but as soon as the conversation concerned himself he would begin to talk circumstantially and with evident satisfaction.

"Consider my position, Peter Nikoláevich. Were I in the cavalry I should get not more than two hundred rubles every four months, even with the rank of lieutenant; but as it is I receive two hundred and thirty," said he, looking at Shinshín and the count with a joyful, pleasant smile, as if it were obvious to him that his success must always be the chief desire of everyone else.

"Besides that, Peter Nikoláevich, by exchanging into the Guards I shall be in a more prominent position," continued Berg, "and vacancies occur much more frequently in the Foot Guards. Then just think what can be done with two hundred and thirty rubles! I even manage to put a little aside and to send something to my father," he went on, emitting a smoke ring.

"*La balance y est...* * A German knows how to skin a flint, as the proverb says," remarked Shinshín, moving his pipe to the other side of his mouth and winking at the count.

* So that squares matters.

The count burst out laughing. The other guests seeing that Shinshín was talking came up to listen. Berg, oblivious of irony or indifference, continued to explain how by exchanging into the Guards he had already gained a step on his old comrades of the Cadet Corps; how in wartime the company commander might get killed and he, as senior in the company, might easily succeed to the post; how popular he was with everyone in the regiment, and how satisfied his father was with him. Berg evidently enjoyed narrating all this, and did not seem to suspect that others, too, might have their own interests. But all he said was so prettily sedate, and the naïveté of his youthful egotism was so obvious, that he disarmed his hearers.

"Well, my boy, you'll get along wherever you go—foot or horse—that I'll warrant," said Shinshín, patting him on the shoulder and taking his feet off the sofa.

Berg smiled joyously. The count, followed by his guests, went into the drawing room.

It was just the moment before a big dinner when the assembled guests, expecting the summons to *zakúska*, * avoid engaging in any long conversation but think it necessary to move about and talk, in order to show that they are not at all impatient for their food. The host and hostess look toward the door, and now and then glance at one another, and the visitors try to guess from these glances who, or what, they are waiting for—some important relation who has not yet arrived, or a dish that is not yet ready.

* Hors d'oeuvres.

Pierre had come just at dinnertime and was sitting awkwardly in the middle of the drawing room on the first chair he had come across, blocking the way for everyone. The countess tried to make him talk, but he went on naïvely looking around through his spectacles as if in search of somebody and answered all her questions in monosyllables. He was in the way and was the only one who did not notice the fact. Most of the guests, knowing of the affair with the bear, looked with curiosity at this big, stout, quiet man, wondering how such a clumsy, modest fellow could have played such a prank on a policeman.

"You have only lately arrived?" the countess asked him.

"*Oui, madame,*" replied he, looking around him.

"You have not yet seen my husband?"

"*Non, madame.*" He smiled quite inappropriately.

"You have been in Paris recently, I believe? I suppose it's very interesting."

"Very interesting."

The countess exchanged glances with Anna Mikháylovna. The latter understood that she was being asked to entertain this young man, and sitting down beside him she began to speak about his father; but he answered her, as he had the countess, only in monosyllables. The other guests were all conversing with one another. "The Razumóvskis... It was charming... You are very kind... Countess Apráksina..." was heard on all sides. The countess rose and went into the ballroom.

"MáryaDmítrievna?" came her voice from there.

"Herself," came the answer in a rough voice, and MáryaDmítrievna entered the room.

All the unmarried ladies and even the married ones except the very oldest rose. MáryaDmítrievna paused at the door. Tall and stout, holding high her fifty-year-old head with its gray curls, she stood surveying the guests, and leisurely arranged her wide sleeves as if rolling them up. MáryaDmítrievna always spoke in Russian.

"Health and happiness to her whose name day we are keeping and to her children," she said, in her loud, full-toned voice which drowned all others. "Well, you old sinner," she went on, turning to the count who was kissing her hand, "you're feeling dull in Moscow, I daresay? Nowhere to hunt with your dogs? But what is to be done, old man? Just see how these nestlings are growing up," and she pointed to the girls. "You must look for husbands for them whether you like it or not...."

"Well," said she, "how's my Cossack?" (MáryaDmítrievna always called Natásha a Cossack) and she stroked the child's arm as she came up fearless and gay to kiss her hand. "I know she's a scamp of a girl, but I like her."

She took a pair of pear-shaped ruby earrings from her huge reticule and, having given them to the rosy Natásha, who beamed with the pleasure of her saint's-day fete, turned away at once and addressed herself to Pierre.

"Eh, eh, friend! Come here a bit," said she, assuming a soft high tone of voice. "Come here, my friend..." and she ominously tucked up her sleeves still higher. Pierre approached, looking at her in a childlike way through his spectacles.

"Come nearer, come nearer, friend! I used to be the only one to tell your father the truth when he was in favor, and in your case it's my evident duty." She paused. All were silent, expectant of what was to follow, for this was clearly only a prelude.

"A fine lad! My word! A fine lad!... His father lies on his deathbed and he amuses himself setting a policeman astride a bear! For shame, sir, for shame! It would be better if you went to the war."

She turned away and gave her hand to the count, who could hardly keep from laughing.

"Well, I suppose it is time we were at table?" said Márya Dmítrievna.

The count went in first with Márya Dmítrievna, the countess followed on the arm of a colonel of hussars, a man of importance to them because Nicholas was to go with him to the regiment; then came Anna Mikháylovna with Shinshín. Berg gave his arm to Véra. The smiling Julie Karágina went in with Nicholas. After them other couples followed, filling the whole dining hall, and last of all the children, tutors, and governesses followed singly. The footmen began moving about, chairs scraped, the band struck up in the gallery, and the guests settled down in their places. Then the strains of the count's household band were replaced by the clatter of knives and forks, the voices of visitors, and the soft steps of the footmen. At one end of the table sat the countess with Márya Dmítrievna on her right and Anna Mikháylovna on her left, the other lady visitors were farther down. At the other end sat the count, with the hussar colonel on his left and Shinshín and the other male visitors on his right. Midway down the long table on one side sat the grown-up young people: Véra beside Berg, and Pierre beside Borís; and on the other side, the children, tutors, and governesses. From behind the crystal decanters and fruit vases, the count kept glancing at his wife and her tall cap with its light-blue ribbons, and busily filled his neighbors' glasses, not neglecting his own. The countess in turn, without omitting her duties as hostess, threw significant glances from behind the pineapples at her husband whose face and bald head seemed by their redness to contrast more than usual with his gray hair. At the ladies' end an even chatter of voices was heard all the time, at the men's end the voices sounded louder and louder, especially that of the colonel of hussars who, growing more and more flushed, ate and drank so much that the count held him up as a pattern to the other guests. Berg with tender smiles was saying to Véra that love is not an earthly but a heavenly feeling. Borís was telling his new friend Pierre who the guests were and exchanging glances with Natásha, who was sitting opposite. Pierre spoke little but examined the new faces, and ate a great deal. Of the two soups he chose turtle with savory patties and went on to the game without omitting a single dish or one of the wines. These latter the butler thrust mysteriously forward, wrapped in a napkin, from behind the next man's shoulders and whispered: "Dry Madeira"... "Hungarian"... or "Rhine wine" as the case might be. Of the four crystal glasses engraved with the count's monogram that stood before his plate, Pierre held out one at random and drank with enjoyment, gazing with ever-increasing amiability at the other guests. Natásha, who sat opposite, was looking at Borís as girls of thirteen look at the boy they are in love with and have just kissed for the first time. Sometimes that same look fell on Pierre, and that funny lively little girl's look made him inclined to laugh without knowing why.

Nicholas sat at some distance from Sónya, beside Julie Karágina, to whom he was again talking with the same involuntary smile. Sónya wore a company smile but was evidently tormented by jealousy; now she turned pale, now blushed and strained every nerve to overhear what Nicholas and Julie were saying to one another. The governess kept looking round uneasily as if preparing to resent any slight that might be put upon the children. The German tutor was trying to remember all the dishes, wines, and kinds of dessert, in order to send a full description of the dinner to his people in Germany; and he felt greatly offended when the butler with a bottle wrapped in a napkin passed him by. He frowned, trying to appear as if he did not want any of that wine, but was mortified because no one would understand that it was not to quench his thirst or from greediness that he wanted it, but simply from a conscientious desire for knowledge.

CHAPTER XIX

At the men's end of the table the talk grew more and more animated. The colonel told them that the declaration of war had already appeared in Petersburg and that a copy, which he had himself seen, had that day been forwarded by courier to the commander in chief.

"And why the deuce are we going to fight Bonaparte?" remarked Shinshín. "He has stopped Austria's cackle and I fear it will be our turn next."

The colonel was a stout, tall, plethoric German, evidently devoted to the service and patriotically Russian. He resented Shinshín's remark.

"It is for the reasson, my goot sir," said he, speaking with a German accent, "for the reassonzatze Emperor knows zat. He declares in zemanifesstozat he cannot fiew wiz indifference ze danger vreatening Russia and zatze safety and dignity of ze Empire as vell as ze sanctity of its *alliances*..." he spoke this last word with particular emphasis as if in it lay the gist of the matter.

Then with the unerring official memory that characterized him he repeated from the opening words of the manifesto:

... and the wish, which constitutes the Emperor's sole and absolute aim—to establish peace in Europe on firm foundations—has now decided him to despatch part of the army abroad and to create a new condition for the attainment of that purpose.

"Zat, my dear sir, is vy..." he concluded, drinking a tumbler of wine with dignity and looking to the count for approval.

"*Connaissez-vous le Proverbe:** 'Jerome, Jerome, do not roam, but turn spindles at home!'?" said Shinshín, puckering his brows and smiling. "*Cela nous convient à merveille.**(2) Suvórov now—he knew what he was about; yet they beat him *à plate couture,**(3) and where are we to find Suvórovs now? *Je vousdemande un peu,*" *(4) said he, continually changing from French to Russian.

* Do you know the proverb?

*(2) That suits us down to the ground.

*(3) Hollow.

*(4) I just ask you that.

"Ve must vight to the last tr-r-op of our plood!" said the colonel, thumping the table; "and ve must tie for our Emperor, and zen all vill pe vell. And ve must discuss it as little as po-o-ossible"... he dwelt particularly on the word *possible*... "as po-o-ossible," he ended, again turning to the count. "Zat is how ve old hussars look at it, and zere's an end of it! And how do you, a young man and a young hussar, how do you judge of it?" he added, addressing Nicholas, who when he heard that the war was being discussed had turned from his partner with eyes and ears intent on the colonel.

"I am quite of your opinion," replied Nicholas, flaming up, turning his plate round and moving his wineglasses about with as much decision and desperation as though he were at that moment facing some great danger. "I am convinced that we Russians must die or conquer," he concluded, conscious—as were others—after the words were uttered that his remarks were too enthusiastic and emphatic for the occasion and were therefore awkward.

"What you said just now was splendid!" said his partner Julie.

Sónya trembled all over and blushed to her ears and behind them and down to her neck and shoulders while Nicholas was speaking.

Pierre listened to the colonel's speech and nodded approvingly.

"That's fine," said he.

"The young man's a real hussar!" shouted the colonel, again thumping the table.

"What are you making such a noise about over there?" MáryaDmítrievna's deep voice suddenly inquired from the other end of the table. "What are you thumping the table for?" she demanded of the hussar, "and why are you exciting yourself? Do you think the French are here?"

"I am speaking ze truce," replied the hussar with a smile.

"It's all about the war," the count shouted down the table. "You know my son's going, MáryaDmítrievna? My son is going."

"I have four sons in the army but still I don't fret. It is all in God's hands. You may die in your bed or God may spare you in a battle," replied MáryaDmítrievna's deep voice, which easily carried the whole length of the table.

"That's true!"

Once more the conversations concentrated, the ladies' at the one end and the men's at the other.

"You won't ask," Natásha's little brother was saying; "I know you won't ask!"

"I will," replied Natásha.

Her face suddenly flushed with reckless and joyous resolution. She half rose, by a glance inviting Pierre, who sat opposite, to listen to what was coming, and turning to her mother:

"Mamma!" rang out the clear contralto notes of her childish voice, audible the whole length of the table.

"What is it?" asked the countess, startled; but seeing by her daughter's face that it was only mischief, she shook a finger at her sternly with a threatening and forbidding movement of her head.

The conversation was hushed.

"Mamma! What sweets are we going to have?" and Natásha's voice sounded still more firm and resolute.

The countess tried to frown, but could not. MáryaDmítrievna shook her fat finger.

"Cossack!" she said threateningly.

Most of the guests, uncertain how to regard this sally, looked at the elders.

"You had better take care!" said the countess.

"Mamma! What sweets are we going to have?" Natásha again cried boldly, with saucy gaiety, confident that her prank would be taken in good part.

Sónya and fat little Pétya doubled up with laughter.

"You see! I *have* asked," whispered Natásha to her little brother and to Pierre, glancing at him again.

"Ice pudding, but you won't get any," said MáryaDmítrievna.

Natásha saw there was nothing to be afraid of and so she braved even MáryaDmítrievna.

"MáryaDmítrievna! What kind of ice pudding? I don't like ice cream."

"Carrot ices."

"No! What kind, MáryaDmítrievna? What kind?" she almost screamed; "I want to know!"

MáryaDmítrievna and the countess burst out laughing, and all the guests joined in. Everyone laughed, not at MáryaDmítrievna's answer but at the incredible boldness and smartness of this little girl who had dared to treat MáryaDmítrievna in this fashion.

Natásha only desisted when she had been told that there would be pineapple ice. Before the ices, champagne was served round. The band again struck up, the count and countess kissed, and the guests, leaving their seats, went up to "congratulate" the countess, and reached across the table to clink glasses with the count, with the children, and with one another. Again the footmen rushed about, chairs scraped, and in the same order in which they had entered but with redder faces, the guests returned to the drawing room and to the count's study.

CHAPTER XX

The card tables were drawn out, sets made up for boston, and the count's visitors settled themselves, some in the two drawing rooms, some in the sitting room, some in the library.

The count, holding his cards fanwise, kept himself with difficulty from dropping into his usual after-dinner nap, and laughed at everything. The young people, at the countess' instigation, gathered round the clavichord and harp. Julie by general request played first. After she had played a little air with variations on the harp, she joined the other young ladies in begging Natásha and Nicholas, who were noted for their musical talent, to sing something. Natásha, who was treated as though she were grown up, was evidently very proud of this but at the same time felt shy.

"What shall we sing?" she said.

"'The Brook,'" suggested Nicholas.

"Well, then, let's be quick. Borís, come here," said Natásha. "But where is Sónya?"

She looked round and seeing that her friend was not in the room ran to look for her.

Running into Sónya's room and not finding her there, Natásha ran to the nursery, but Sónya was not there either. Natásha concluded that she must be on the chest in the passage. The chest in the passage was the place of mourning for the younger female generation in the Rostóv household. And there in fact was Sónya lying face downward on Nurse's dirty feather bed on the top of the chest, crumpling her gauzy pink dress under her, hiding her face with her slender fingers, and sobbing so convulsively that her bare little shoulders shook. Natásha's face, which had been so radiantly happy all that saint's day, suddenly changed: her eyes became fixed, and then a shiver passed down her broad neck and the corners of her mouth drooped.

"Sónya! What is it? What is the matter?... Oo... Oo... Oo...!" And Natásha's large mouth widened, making her look quite ugly, and she began to wail like a baby without knowing why, except that Sónya was crying. Sónya tried to lift her head to answer but could not, and hid her face still deeper in the bed. Natásha wept, sitting on the blue-striped feather bed and hugging her friend. With an effort Sónya sat up and began wiping her eyes and explaining.

"Nicholas is going away in a week's time, his... papers... have come... he told me himself... but still I should not cry," and she showed a paper she held in her hand—with the verses Nicholas had written, "still, I should not cry, but you can't... no one can understand... what a soul he has!"

And she began to cry again because he had such a noble soul.

"It's all very well for you... I am not envious... I love you and Borís also," she went on, gaining a little strength; "he is nice... there are no difficulties in your way.... But Nicholas is my cousin... one would have to... the Metropolitan himself... and even then it can't be done. And besides, if she tells Mamma" (Sónya looked upon the countess as her mother and called her so) "that I am spoiling Nicholas' career and am heartless and ungrateful, while truly... God is my witness," and she made the sign of the cross, "I love her so much, and all of you, only Véra... And what for? What have I done to her? I am so grateful to you that I would willingly sacrifice everything, only I have nothing...."

Sónya could not continue, and again hid her face in her hands and in the feather bed. Natásha began consoling her, but her face showed that she understood all the gravity of her friend's trouble.

"Sónya," she suddenly exclaimed, as if she had guessed the true reason of her friend's sorrow, "I'm sure Véra has said something to you since dinner? Hasn't she?"

"Yes, these verses Nicholas wrote himself and I copied some others, and she found them on my table and said she'd show them to Mamma, and that I was ungrateful, and that Mamma would never allow him to marry me, but that he'll marry Julie. You see how he's been with her all day... Natásha, what have I done to deserve it?..."

And again she began to sob, more bitterly than before. Natásha lifted her up, hugged her, and, smiling through her tears, began comforting her.

"Sónya, don't believe her, darling! Don't believe her! Do you remember how we and Nicholas, all three of us, talked in the sitting room after supper? Why, we settled how everything was to be. I don't quite remember how, but don't you remember that it could all be arranged and how nice it all was? There's Uncle Shinshín's brother has married his first cousin. And we are only second cousins, you know. And Borís says it is quite possible. You know I have told him all about it. And he is so clever and so good!" said Natásha. "Don't you cry, Sónya, dear love, darling Sónya!" and she kissed her and laughed. "Véra's spiteful; never mind her! And all will come right and she won't say anything to Mamma. Nicholas will tell her himself, and he doesn't care at all for Julie."

Natásha kissed her on the hair.

Sónya sat up. The little kitten brightened, its eyes shone, and it seemed ready to lift its tail, jump down on its soft paws, and begin playing with the ball of worsted as a kitten should.

"Do you think so?... Really? Truly?" she said, quickly smoothing her frock and hair.

"Really, truly!" answered Natásha, pushing in a crisp lock that had strayed from under her friend's plaits.

Both laughed.

"Well, let's go and sing 'The Brook.'"

"Come along!"

"Do you know, that fat Pierre who sat opposite me is so funny!" said Natásha, stopping suddenly. "I feel so happy!"

And she set off at a run along the passage.

Sónya, shaking off some down which clung to her and tucking away the verses in the bosom of her dress close to her bony little chest, ran after Natásha down the passage into the sitting room with flushed face and light, joyous steps. At the visitors' request the young people sang the quartette, "The Brook," with which everyone was delighted. Then Nicholas sang a song he had just learned:

At nighttime in the moon's fair glow How sweet, as fancies wander free, To feel that in this world there's one Who still is thinking but of thee! That while her fingers touch the harp Wafting sweet music o'er the lea, It is for thee thus swells her heart, Sighing its message out to thee... A day or two, then bliss unspoilt, But oh! till then I cannot live!...

He had not finished the last verse before the young people began to get ready to dance in the large hall, and the sound of the feet and the coughing of the musicians were heard from the gallery.

Pierre was sitting in the drawing room where Shinshín had engaged him, as a man recently returned from abroad, in a political conversation in which several others joined but which bored Pierre. When the music began Natásha came in and walking straight up to Pierre said, laughing and blushing:

"Mamma told me to ask you to join the dancers."

"I am afraid of mixing the figures," Pierre replied; "but if you will be my teacher..." And lowering his big arm he offered it to the slender little girl.

While the couples were arranging themselves and the musicians tuning up, Pierre sat down with his little partner. Natásha was perfectly happy; she was dancing with a *grown-up* man, who had been *abroad*. She was sitting in a conspicuous place and talking to him like a grown-up lady. She had a fan in her hand that one of the ladies had given her to hold. Assuming quite the pose of a society woman (heaven knows when and where she had learned it) she talked with her partner, fanning herself and smiling over the fan.

"Dear, dear! Just look at her!" exclaimed the countess as she crossed the ballroom, pointing to Natásha.

Natásha blushed and laughed.

"Well, really, Mamma! Why should you? What is there to be surprised at?"

In the midst of the third *écossaise* there was a clatter of chairs being pushed back in the sitting room where the count and MáryaDmítrievna had been playing cards with the majority of the more distinguished and older visitors. They now, stretching themselves after sitting so long, and replacing their purses and pocketbooks, entered the ballroom. First came MáryaDmítrievna and the count, both with merry countenances. The count, with playful ceremony somewhat in ballet style, offered his bent arm to

MáryaDmítrievna. He drew himself up, a smile of debonair gallantry lit up his face and as soon as the last figure of the *écossaise* was ended, he clapped his hands to the musicians and shouted up to their gallery, addressing the first violin:

"Semën! Do you know the *Daniel Cooper?*"

This was the count's favorite dance, which he had danced in his youth. (Strictly speaking, *Daniel Cooper* was one figure of the *anglaise*.)

"Look at Papa!" shouted Natásha to the whole company, and quite forgetting that she was dancing with a grown-up partner she bent her curly head to her knees and made the whole room ring with her laughter.

And indeed everybody in the room looked with a smile of pleasure at the jovial old gentleman, who standing beside his tall and stout partner, MáryaDmítrievna, curved his arms, beat time, straightened his shoulders, turned out his toes, tapped gently with his foot, and, by a smile that broadened his round face more and more, prepared the onlookers for what was to follow. As soon as the provocatively gay strains of *Daniel Cooper* (somewhat resembling those of a merry peasant dance) began to sound, all the doorways of the ballroom were suddenly filled by the domestic serfs—the men on one side and the women on the other—who with beaming faces had come to see their master making merry.

"Just look at the master! A regular eagle he is!" loudly remarked the nurse, as she stood in one of the doorways.

The count danced well and knew it. But his partner could not and did not want to dance well. Her enormous figure stood erect, her powerful arms hanging down (she had handed her reticule to the countess), and only her stern but handsome face really joined in the dance. What was expressed by the whole of the count's plump figure, in MáryaDmítrievna found expression only in her more and more beaming face and quivering nose. But if the count, getting more and more into the swing of it, charmed the spectators by the unexpectedness of his adroit maneuvers and the agility with which he capered about on his light feet, MáryaDmítrievna produced no less impression by slight exertions—the least effort to move her shoulders or bend her arms when turning, or stamp her foot—which everyone appreciated in view of her size and habitual severity. The dance grew livelier and livelier. The other couples could not attract a moment's attention to their own evolutions and did not even try to do so. All were watching the count and MáryaDmítrievna. Natásha kept pulling everyone by sleeve or dress, urging them to "look at Papa!" though as it was they never took their eyes off the couple. In the intervals of the dance the count, breathing deeply, waved and shouted to the musicians to play faster. Faster, faster, and faster; lightly, more lightly, and yet more lightly whirled the count, flying round MáryaDmítrievna, now on his toes, now on his heels; until, turning his partner round to her seat, he executed the final *pas*, raising his soft foot backwards, bowing his perspiring head, smiling and making a wide sweep with his arm, amid a thunder of applause and laughter led by Natásha. Both partners stood still, breathing heavily and wiping their faces with their cambric handkerchiefs.

"That's how we used to dance in our time, *ma chère*," said the count.

"That *was* a *Daniel Cooper!*" exclaimed MáryaDmítrievna, tucking up her sleeves and puffing heavily.

CHAPTER XXI

While in the Rostóvs' ballroom the sixth *anglaise* was being danced, to a tune in which the weary musicians blundered, and while tired footmen and cooks were getting the supper, Count Bezúkhov had a sixth stroke. The doctors pronounced recovery impossible. After a mute confession, communion was administered to the dying man, preparations made for the sacrament of unction, and in his house there was the bustle and thrill of suspense usual at such moments. Outside the house, beyond the gates, a group of undertakers, who hid whenever a carriage drove up, waited in expectation of an important order for an expensive funeral. The Military Governor of Moscow, who had been assiduous in sending aides-de-camp to inquire after the count's health, came himself that evening to bid a last farewell to the celebrated grandee of Catherine's court, Count Bezúkhov.

The magnificent reception room was crowded. Everyone stood up respectfully when the Military Governor, having stayed about half an hour alone with the dying man, passed out, slightly acknowledging their bows and trying to escape as quickly as possible from the glances fixed on him by the doctors, clergy, and relatives of the family. Prince Vasíli, who had grown thinner and paler during the last few days, escorted him to the door, repeating something to him several times in low tones.

When the Military Governor had gone, Prince Vasíli sat down all alone on a chair in the ballroom, crossing one leg high over the other, leaning his elbow on his knee and covering his face with his hand. After sitting so for a while he rose, and, looking about him with frightened eyes, went with unusually hurried steps down the long corridor leading to the back of the house, to the room of the eldest princess.

Those who were in the dimly lit reception room spoke in nervous whispers, and, whenever anyone went into or came from the dying man's room, grew silent and gazed with eyes full of curiosity or expectancy at his door, which creaked slightly when opened.

"The limits of human life ... are fixed and may not be o'erpassed," said an old priest to a lady who had taken a seat beside him and was listening naïvely to his words.

"I wonder, is it not too late to administer unction?" asked the lady, adding the priest's clerical title, as if she had no opinion of her own on the subject.

"Ah, madam, it is a great sacrament," replied the priest, passing his hand over the thin grizzled strands of hair combed back across his bald head.

"Who was that? The Military Governor himself?" was being asked at the other side of the room. "How young-looking he is!"

"Yes, and he is over sixty. I hear the count no longer recognizes anyone. They wished to administer the sacrament of unction."

"I knew someone who received that sacrament seven times."

The second princess had just come from the sickroom with her eyes red from weeping and sat down beside Dr. Lorrain, who was sitting in a graceful pose under a portrait of Catherine, leaning his elbow on a table.

"Beautiful," said the doctor in answer to a remark about the weather. "The weather is beautiful, Princess; and besides, in Moscow one feels as if one were in the country."

"Yes, indeed," replied the princess with a sigh. "So he may have something to drink?"

Lorrain considered.

"Has he taken his medicine?"

"Yes."

The doctor glanced at his watch.

"Take a glass of boiled water and put a pinch of cream of tartar," and he indicated with his delicate fingers what he meant by a pinch.

"Dere has neffer been a gase," a German doctor was saying to an aide-de-camp, "dat one liffs after de sird stroke."

"And what a well-preserved man he was!" remarked the aide-de-camp. "And who will inherit his wealth?" he added in a whisper.

"It von't go begging," replied the German with a smile.

Everyone again looked toward the door, which creaked as the second princess went in with the drink she had prepared according to Lorrain's instructions. The German doctor went up to Lorrain.

"Do you think he can last till morning?" asked the German, addressing Lorrain in French which he pronounced badly.

Lorrain, pursing up his lips, waved a severely negative finger before his nose.

"Tonight, not later," said he in a low voice, and he moved away with a decorous smile of self-satisfaction at being able clearly to understand and state the patient's condition.

Meanwhile Prince Vasíli had opened the door into the princess' room.

In this room it was almost dark; only two tiny lamps were burning before the icons and there was a pleasant scent of flowers and burnt pastilles. The room was crowded with small pieces of furniture, whatnots, cupboards, and little tables. The quilt of a high, white feather bed was just visible behind a screen. A small dog began to bark.

"Ah, is it you, cousin?"

She rose and smoothed her hair, which was as usual so extremely smooth that it seemed to be made of one piece with her head and covered with varnish.

"Has anything happened?" she asked. "I am so terrified."

"No, there is no change. I only came to have a talk about business, Catiche," * muttered the prince, seating himself wearily on the chair she had just vacated. "You have made the place warm, I must say," he remarked. "Well, sit down: let's have a talk."

* Catherine.

"I thought perhaps something had happened," she said with her unchanging stonily severe expression; and, sitting down opposite the prince, she prepared to listen.

"I wished to get a nap, *mon cousin*, but I can't."

"Well, my dear?" said Prince Vasíli, taking her hand and bending it downwards as was his habit.

It was plain that this "well?" referred to much that they both understood without naming.

The princess, who had a straight, rigid body, abnormally long for her legs, looked directly at Prince Vasíli with no sign of emotion in her prominent gray eyes. Then she shook her head and glanced up at the icons with a sigh. This might have been taken as an expression of sorrow and devotion, or of weariness and hope of resting before long. Prince Vasíli understood it as an expression of weariness.

"And I?" he said; "do you think it is easier for me? I am as worn out as a post horse, but still I must have a talk with you, Catiche, a very serious talk."

Prince Vasíli said no more and his cheeks began to twitch nervously, now on one side, now on the other, giving his face an unpleasant expression which was never to be seen on it in a drawing room. His eyes too seemed strange; at one moment they looked impudently sly and at the next glanced round in alarm.

The princess, holding her little dog on her lap with her thin bony hands, looked attentively into Prince Vasíli's eyes evidently resolved not to be the first to break silence, if she had to wait till morning.

"Well, you see, my dear princess and cousin, Catherine Semënovna," continued Prince Vasíli, returning to his theme, apparently not without an inner struggle; "at such a moment as this one must think of everything. One must think of the future, of all of you... I love you all, like children of my own, as you know."

The princess continued to look at him without moving, and with the same dull expression.

"And then of course my family has also to be considered," Prince Vasíli went on, testily pushing away a little table without looking at her. "You know, Catiche, that we—you three sisters, Mámontov, and my wife—are the count's only direct heirs. I know, I know how hard it is for you to talk or think of such matters. It is no easier for me; but, my dear, I am getting on for sixty and must be prepared for anything. Do you know I have sent for Pierre? The count," pointing to his portrait, "definitely demanded that he should be called."

Prince Vasíli looked questioningly at the princess, but could not make out whether she was considering what he had just said or whether she was simply looking at him.

"There is one thing I constantly pray God to grant, *mon cousin*," she replied, "and it is that He would be merciful to him and would allow his noble soul peacefully to leave this..."

"Yes, yes, of course," interrupted Prince Vasíli impatiently, rubbing his bald head and angrily pulling back toward him the little table that he had pushed away. "But... in short, the fact is... you know yourself that last winter the count made a will by which he left all his property, not to us his direct heirs, but to Pierre."

"He has made wills enough!" quietly remarked the princess. "But he cannot leave the estate to Pierre. Pierre is illegitimate."

"But, my dear," said Prince Vasíli suddenly, clutching the little table and becoming more animated and talking more rapidly: "what if a letter has been written to the Emperor in which the count asks for Pierre's legitimation? Do you understand that in consideration of the count's services, his request would be granted?..."

The princess smiled as people do who think they know more about the subject under discussion than those they are talking with.

"I can tell you more," continued Prince Vasíli, seizing her hand, "that letter was written, though it was not sent, and the Emperor knew of it. The only question is, has it been destroyed or not? If not, then as soon as *all is over*," and Prince Vasíli sighed to intimate what he meant by the words *all is over*, "and the count's papers are opened, the will and letter will be delivered to the Emperor, and the petition will certainly be granted. Pierre will get everything as the legitimate son."

"And our share?" asked the princess smiling ironically, as if anything might happen, only not that.

"But, my poor Catiche, it is as clear as daylight! He will then be the legal heir to everything and you won't get anything. You must know, my dear, whether the will and letter were written, and whether they have been destroyed or not. And if they have somehow been overlooked, you ought to know where they are, and must find them, because..."

"What next?" the princess interrupted, smiling sardonically and not changing the expression of her eyes. "I am a woman, and you think we are all stupid; but I know this: an illegitimate son cannot inherit... *un bâtard!*"* she added, as if supposing that this translation of the word would effectively prove to Prince Vasíli the invalidity of his contention.

* A bastard.

"Well, really, Catiche! Can't you understand! You are so intelligent, how is it you don't see that if the count has written a letter to the Emperor begging him to recognize Pierre as legitimate, it follows that Pierre will not be Pierre but will become Count Bezúkhov, and will then inherit everything under the will? And if the will and letter are not destroyed, then you will have nothing but the consolation of having been dutiful *et tout ce qui s'ensuit!** That's certain."

* And all that follows therefrom.

"I know the will was made, but I also know that it is invalid; and you, *mon cousin*, seem to consider me a perfect fool," said the princess with the expression women assume when they suppose they are saying something witty and stinging.

"My dear Princess Catherine Semënovna," began Prince Vasíli impatiently, "I came here not to wrangle with you, but to talk about your interests as with a kinswoman, a good, kind, true relation. And I tell you for the tenth time that if the letter to the Emperor and the will in Pierre's favor are among the count's papers, then, my dear girl, you and your sisters are not heiresses! If you don't believe me, then believe an expert. I have just been talking to DmítriOnúfrich" (the family solicitor) "and he says the same."

At this a sudden change evidently took place in the princess' ideas; her thin lips grew white, though her eyes did not change, and her voice when she began to speak passed through such transitions as she herself evidently did not expect.

"That would be a fine thing!" said she. "I never wanted anything and I don't now."

She pushed the little dog off her lap and smoothed her dress.

"And this is gratitude—this is recognition for those who have sacrificed everything for his sake!" she cried. "It's splendid! Fine! I don't want anything, Prince."

"Yes, but you are not the only one. There are your sisters..." replied Prince Vasíli.

But the princess did not listen to him.

"Yes, I knew it long ago but had forgotten. I knew that I could expect nothing but meanness, deceit, envy, intrigue, and ingratitude—the blackest ingratitude—in this house..."

"Do you or do you not know where that will is?" insisted Prince Vasíli, his cheeks twitching more than ever.

"Yes, I was a fool! I still believed in people, loved them, and sacrificed myself. But only the base, the vile succeed! I know who has been intriguing!"

The princess wished to rise, but the prince held her by the hand. She had the air of one who has suddenly lost faith in the whole human race. She gave her companion an angry glance.

"There is still time, my dear. You must remember, Catiche, that it was all done casually in a moment of anger, of illness, and was afterwards forgotten. Our duty, my dear, is to rectify his mistake, to ease his last moments by not letting him commit this injustice, and not to let him die feeling that he is rendering unhappy those who..."

"Who sacrificed everything for him," chimed in the princess, who would again have risen had not the prince still held her fast, "though he never could appreciate it. No, *mon cousin*," she added with a sigh, "I shall always remember that in this world one must expect no reward, that in this world there is neither honor nor justice. In this world one has to be cunning and cruel."

"Now come, come! Be reasonable. I know your excellent heart."

"No, I have a wicked heart."

"I know your heart," repeated the prince. "I value your friendship and wish you to have as good an opinion of me. Don't upset yourself, and let us talk sensibly while there is still time, be it a day or be it but an hour.... Tell me all you know about the will, and above all where it is. You must know. We will take it at once and show it to the count. He has, no doubt, forgotten it and will wish to destroy it. You understand that my sole desire is conscientiously to carry out his wishes; that is my only reason for being here. I came simply to help him and you."

"Now I see it all! I know who has been intriguing—I know!" cried the princess.

"That's not the point, my dear."

"It's that protégé of yours, that sweet Princess Drubetskáya, that Anna Mikháylovna whom I would not take for a housemaid... the infamous, vile woman!"

"Do not let us lose any time..."

"Ah, don't talk to me! Last winter she wheedled herself in here and told the count such vile, disgraceful things about us, especially about Sophie—I can't repeat them—that it made the count quite ill and he would not see us for a whole fortnight. I know it was then he wrote this vile, infamous paper, but I thought the thing was invalid."

"We've got to it at last—why did you not tell me about it sooner?"

"It's in the inlaid portfolio that he keeps under his pillow," said the princess, ignoring his question. "Now I know! Yes; if I have a sin, a great sin, it is hatred of that vile woman!" almost shrieked the princess, now quite changed. "And what does she come worming herself in here for? But I will give her a piece of my mind. The time will come!"

CHAPTER XXII

While these conversations were going on in the reception room and the princess' room, a carriage containing Pierre (who had been sent for) and Anna Mikháylovna (who found it necessary to accompany him) was driving into the court of Count Bezúkhov's house. As the wheels rolled softly over the straw beneath the windows, Anna Mikháylovna, having turned with words of comfort to her companion, realized that he was asleep in his corner and woke him up. Rousing himself, Pierre followed Anna Mikháylovna out of the carriage, and only then began to think of the interview with his dying father which awaited him. He noticed that they had not come to the front entrance but to the back door. While he was getting down from the carriage steps two men, who looked like tradespeople, ran hurriedly from the entrance and hid in the shadow of the wall. Pausing for a moment, Pierre noticed several other men of the same kind hiding in the shadow of the house on both sides. But neither Anna Mikháylovna nor the footman nor the coachman, who could not help seeing these people, took any notice of them. "It seems to be all right," Pierre concluded, and followed Anna Mikháylovna. She hurriedly ascended the narrow dimly lit stone staircase, calling to Pierre, who was lagging behind, to follow. Though he did not see why it was necessary for him to go to the count at all, still less why he had to go by the back stairs, yet judging by Anna Mikháylovna's air of assurance and haste, Pierre concluded that it was all absolutely necessary. Halfway up the stairs they were almost knocked over by some men who, carrying pails, came running downstairs, their boots clattering. These men pressed close to the wall to let Pierre and Anna Mikháylovna pass and did not evince the least surprise at seeing them there.

"Is this the way to the princesses' apartments?" asked Anna Mikháylovna of one of them.

"Yes," replied a footman in a bold loud voice, as if anything were now permissible; "the door to the left, ma'am."

"Perhaps the count did not ask for me," said Pierre when he reached the landing. "I'd better go to my own room."

Anna Mikháylovna paused and waited for him to come up.

"Ah, my friend!" she said, touching his arm as she had done her son's when speaking to him that afternoon, "believe me I suffer no less than you do, but be a man!"

"But really, hadn't I better go away?" he asked, looking kindly at her over his spectacles.

"Ah, my dear friend! Forget the wrongs that may have been done you. Think that he is your father ... perhaps in the agony of death." She sighed. "I have loved you like a son from the first. Trust yourself to me, Pierre. I shall not forget your interests."

Pierre did not understand a word, but the conviction that all this had to be grew stronger, and he meekly followed Anna Mikháylovna who was already opening a door.

This door led into a back anteroom. An old man, a servant of the princesses, sat in a corner knitting a stocking. Pierre had never been in this part of the house and did not even know of the existence of these rooms. Anna Mikháylovna, addressing a maid who was hurrying past with a decanter on a tray as "my dear" and "my sweet," asked about the princess' health and then led Pierre along a stone passage. The first door on the left led into the princesses' apartments. The maid with the decanter in her haste had not closed the door (everything in the house was done in haste at that time), and Pierre and Anna Mikháylovna in passing instinctively glanced into the room, where Prince Vasíli and the eldest princess were sitting close together talking. Seeing them pass, Prince Vasíli drew back with obvious impatience, while the princess jumped up and with a gesture of desperation slammed the door with all her might.

This action was so unlike her usual composure and the fear depicted on Prince Vasíli's face so out of keeping with his dignity that Pierre stopped and glanced inquiringly over his spectacles at his guide. Anna Mikháylovna evinced no surprise, she only smiled faintly and sighed, as if to say that this was no more than she had expected.

"Be a man, my friend. I will look after your interests," said she in reply to his look, and went still faster along the passage.

Pierre could not make out what it was all about, and still less what "watching over his interests" meant, but he decided that all these things had to be. From the passage they went into a large, dimly lit room adjoining the count's reception room. It was one of those sumptuous but cold apartments known to Pierre only from the front approach, but even in this room there now stood an empty bath, and water had been spilled on the carpet. They were met by a deacon with a censer and by a servant who passed out on tiptoe without heeding them. They went into the reception room familiar to Pierre, with two Italian windows opening into the conservatory, with its large bust and full length portrait of Catherine the Great. The same people were still sitting here in almost the same positions as before, whispering to one another. All became silent and turned to look at the pale tear-worn Anna Mikháylovna as she entered, and at the big stout figure of Pierre who, hanging his head, meekly followed her.

Anna Mikháylovna's face expressed a consciousness that the decisive moment had arrived. With the air of a practical Petersburg lady she now, keeping Pierre close beside her, entered the room even more boldly than that afternoon. She felt that as she brought with her the person the dying man wished to see, her own admission was assured. Casting a rapid glance at all those in the room and noticing the count's confessor there, she glided up to him with a sort of amble, not exactly bowing yet seeming to grow suddenly smaller, and respectfully received the blessing first of one and then of another priest.

"God be thanked that you are in time," said she to one of the priests; "all we relatives have been in such anxiety. This young man is the count's son," she added more softly. "What a terrible moment!"

Having said this she went up to the doctor.

"Dear doctor," said she, "this young man is the count's son. Is there any hope?"

The doctor cast a rapid glance upwards and silently shrugged his shoulders. Anna Mikháylovna with just the same movement raised her shoulders and eyes, almost closing the latter, sighed, and moved away from the doctor to Pierre. To him, in a particularly respectful and tenderly sad voice, she said:

"Trust in His mercy!" and pointing out a small sofa for him to sit and wait for her, she went silently toward the door that everyone was watching and it creaked very slightly as she disappeared behind it.

Pierre, having made up his mind to obey his monitress implicitly, moved toward the sofa she had indicated. As soon as Anna Mikháylovna had disappeared he noticed that the eyes of all in the room turned to him with something more than curiosity and sympathy. He noticed that they whispered to one another, casting significant looks at him with a kind of awe and even servility. A deference such as he had never before received was shown him. A strange lady, the one who had been talking to the priests, rose and offered him her seat; an aide-de-camp picked up and returned a glove Pierre had dropped; the doctors became respectfully silent as he passed by, and moved to make way for him. At first Pierre wished to take another seat so as not to trouble the lady, and also to pick up the glove himself and to pass round the doctors who were not even in his way; but all at once he felt that this would not do, and that tonight he was a person obliged to perform some sort of awful rite which everyone expected of him, and that he was therefore bound to accept their services. He took the glove in silence from the aide-de-camp, and sat down in the lady's chair, placing his huge hands symmetrically on his knees in the naïve attitude of an Egyptian statue, and decided in his own mind that all was as it should be, and that in order not to lose his head and do foolish things he must not act on his own ideas tonight, but must yield himself up entirely to the will of those who were guiding him.

Not two minutes had passed before Prince Vasíli with head erect majestically entered the room. He was wearing his long coat with three stars on his breast. He seemed to have grown thinner since the morning; his eyes seemed larger than usual when he glanced round and noticed Pierre. He went up to him, took his hand (a thing he never used to do), and drew it downwards as if wishing to ascertain whether it was firmly fixed on.

"Courage, courage, my friend! He has asked to see you. That is well!" and he turned to go.

But Pierre thought it necessary to ask: "How is..." and hesitated, not knowing whether it would be proper to call the dying man "the count," yet ashamed to call him "father."

"He had another stroke about half an hour ago. Courage, my friend..."

Pierre's mind was in such a confused state that the word "stroke" suggested to him a blow from something. He looked at Prince Vasíli in perplexity, and only later grasped that a stroke was an attack of illness. Prince Vasíli said something to Lorrain in passing and went through the door on tiptoe. He could not walk well on tiptoe and his whole body jerked at each step. The eldest princess followed him, and the priests and deacons and some servants also went in at the door. Through that door was heard a noise of things being moved about, and at last Anna Mikháylovna, still with the same expression, pale but resolute in the discharge of duty, ran out and touching Pierre lightly on the arm said:

"The divine mercy is inexhaustible! Unction is about to be administered. Come."

Pierre went in at the door, stepping on the soft carpet, and noticed that the strange lady, the aide-de-camp, and some of the servants, all followed him in, as if there were now no further need for permission to enter that room.

CHAPTER XXIII

Pierre well knew this large room divided by columns and an arch, its walls hung round with Persian carpets. The part of the room behind the columns, with a high silk-curtained mahogany bedstead on one side and on the other an immense case containing icons, was brightly illuminated with red light like a Russian church during evening service. Under the gleaming icons stood a long invalid chair, and in that chair on snowy-white smooth pillows, evidently freshly changed, Pierre saw—covered to the waist by a bright green quilt—the familiar, majestic figure of his father, Count Bezúkhov, with that gray mane of hair above his broad forehead which reminded one of a lion, and the deep characteristically noble wrinkles of his handsome, ruddy face. He lay just under the icons; his large thick hands outside the quilt. Into the right hand, which was lying palm downwards, a wax taper had been thrust between forefinger and thumb, and an old servant, bending over from behind the chair, held it in position. By the chair stood the priests, their long hair falling over their magnificent glittering vestments, with lighted tapers in their hands, slowly and solemnly conducting the service. A little behind them stood the two younger princesses holding handkerchiefs to their eyes, and just in front of them their eldest sister, Catiche, with a vicious and determined look steadily fixed on the icons, as though declaring to all that she could not answer for herself should she glance round. Anna Mikháylovna, with a meek, sorrowful, and all-forgiving expression on her face, stood by the door near the strange lady. Prince Vasíli in front of the door, near the invalid chair, a wax taper in his left hand, was leaning his left arm on the carved back of a velvet chair he had turned round for the purpose, and was crossing himself with his right hand, turning his eyes upward each time he touched his forehead. His face wore a calm look of piety and resignation to the will of God. "If you do not understand these sentiments," he seemed to be saying, "so much the worse for you!"

Behind him stood the aide-de-camp, the doctors, and the menservants; the men and women had separated as in church. All were silently crossing themselves, and the reading of the church service, the subdued chanting of deep bass voices, and in the intervals sighs and the shuffling of feet were the only sounds that could be heard. Anna Mikháylovna, with an air of importance that showed that she felt she quite knew what she was about, went across the room to where Pierre was standing and gave him a taper. He lit it and, distracted by observing those around him, began crossing himself with the hand that held the taper.

Sophie, the rosy, laughter-loving, youngest princess with the mole, watched him. She smiled, hid her face in her handkerchief, and remained with it hidden for awhile; then looking up and seeing Pierre she again began to laugh. She evidently felt unable to look at him without laughing, but could not resist looking at him: so to be out of temptation she slipped quietly behind one of the columns. In the midst of the service the voices of the priests suddenly ceased, they whispered to one another, and the old servant who was holding the count's hand got up and said something to the ladies. Anna Mikháylovna stepped forward and, stooping over the dying man, beckoned to Lorrain from behind her back. The French doctor held no taper; he was leaning against one of the columns in a respectful attitude implying that he, a foreigner, in spite of all differences of faith, understood the full importance of the rite now being performed and even approved of it. He now approached the sick man with the noiseless step of one in full vigor of life, with his delicate white fingers raised from the green quilt the hand that was free, and turning sideways felt the pulse and reflected a moment. The sick man was given something to drink, there was a stir around him, then the people resumed their places and the service continued. During this interval Pierre noticed that Prince Vasíli left the chair on which he had been leaning, and—with an air which intimated that he knew what he was about and if others did not understand him it was so much the worse for them—did not go up to the dying man, but passed by him, joined the eldest princess, and moved with her to the side of the room where stood the high bedstead with its silken hangings. On leaving the bed both Prince Vasíli and the princess passed out by a back door, but returned to their places one after the other before the service was concluded. Pierre paid no more attention to this occurrence than to the rest of what went on, having made up his mind once for all that what he saw happening around him that evening was in some way essential.

The chanting of the service ceased, and the voice of the priest was heard respectfully congratulating the dying man on having received the sacrament. The dying man lay as lifeless and immovable as before. Around him everyone began to stir: steps were audible and whispers, among which Anna Mikháylovna's was the most distinct.

Pierre heard her say:

"Certainly he must be moved onto the bed; here it will be impossible..."

The sick man was so surrounded by doctors, princesses, and servants that Pierre could no longer see the reddish-yellow face with its gray mane—which, though he saw other faces as well, he had not lost sight of for a single moment during the whole service. He judged by the cautious movements of those who crowded round the invalid chair that they had lifted the dying man and were moving him.

"Catch hold of my arm or you'll drop him!" he heard one of the servants say in a frightened whisper. "Catch hold from underneath. Here!" exclaimed different voices; and the heavy breathing of the bearers and the shuffling of their feet grew more hurried, as if the weight they were carrying were too much for them.

As the bearers, among whom was Anna Mikháylovna, passed the young man he caught a momentary glimpse between their heads and backs of the dying man's high, stout, uncovered chest and powerful shoulders, raised by those who were holding him under the armpits, and of his gray, curly, leonine head. This head, with its remarkably broad brow and cheekbones, its handsome, sensual mouth, and its cold, majestic expression, was not disfigured by the approach of death. It was the same as Pierre remembered it three months before, when the count had sent him to Petersburg. But now this head was swaying helplessly with the uneven movements of the bearers, and the cold listless gaze fixed itself upon nothing.

After a few minutes' bustle beside the high bedstead, those who had carried the sick man dispersed. Anna Mikháylovna touched

Pierre's hand and said, "Come." Pierre went with her to the bed on which the sick man had been laid in a stately pose in keeping with the ceremony just completed. He lay with his head propped high on the pillows. His hands were symmetrically placed on the green silk quilt, the palms downward. When Pierre came up the count was gazing straight at him, but with a look the significance of which could not be understood by mortal man. Either this look meant nothing but that as long as one has eyes they must look somewhere, or it meant too much. Pierre hesitated, not knowing what to do, and glanced inquiringly at his guide. Anna Mikháylovna made a hurried sign with her eyes, glancing at the sick man's hand and moving her lips as if to send it a kiss. Pierre, carefully stretching his neck so as not to touch the quilt, followed her suggestion and pressed his lips to the large boned, fleshy hand. Neither the hand nor a single muscle of the count's face stirred. Once more Pierre looked questioningly at Anna Mikháylovna to see what he was to do next. Anna Mikháylovna with her eyes indicated a chair that stood beside the bed. Pierre obediently sat down, his eyes asking if he were doing right. Anna Mikháylovna nodded approvingly. Again Pierre fell into the naïvely symmetrical pose of an Egyptian statue, evidently distressed that his stout and clumsy body took up so much room and doing his utmost to look as small as possible. He looked at the count, who still gazed at the spot where Pierre's face had been before he sat down. Anna Mikháylovna indicated by her attitude her consciousness of the pathetic importance of these last moments of meeting between the father and son. This lasted about two minutes, which to Pierre seemed an hour. Suddenly the broad muscles and lines of the count's face began to twitch. The twitching increased, the handsome mouth was drawn to one side (only now did Pierre realize how near death his father was), and from that distorted mouth issued an indistinct, hoarse sound. Anna Mikháylovna looked attentively at the sick man's eyes, trying to guess what he wanted; she pointed first to Pierre, then to some drink, then named Prince Vasíli in an inquiring whisper, then pointed to the quilt. The eyes and face of the sick man showed impatience. He made an effort to look at the servant who stood constantly at the head of the bed.

"Wants to turn on the other side," whispered the servant, and got up to turn the count's heavy body toward the wall.

Pierre rose to help him.

While the count was being turned over, one of his arms fell back helplessly and he made a fruitless effort to pull it forward. Whether he noticed the look of terror with which Pierre regarded that lifeless arm, or whether some other thought flitted across his dying brain, at any rate he glanced at the refractory arm, at Pierre's terror-stricken face, and again at the arm, and on his face a feeble, piteous smile appeared, quite out of keeping with his features, that seemed to deride his own helplessness. At sight of this smile Pierre felt an unexpected quivering in his breast and a tickling in his nose, and tears dimmed his eyes. The sick man was turned on to his side with his face to the wall. He sighed.

"He is dozing," said Anna Mikháylovna, observing that one of the princesses was coming to take her turn at watching. "Let us go."

Pierre went out.

CHAPTER XXIV

There was now no one in the reception room except Prince Vasíli and the eldest princess, who were sitting under the portrait of Catherine the Great and talking eagerly. As soon as they saw Pierre and his companion they became silent, and Pierre thought he saw the princess hide something as she whispered:

"I can't bear the sight of that woman."

"Catiche has had tea served in the small drawing room," said Prince Vasíli to Anna Mikháylovna. "Go and take something, my poor Anna Mikháylovna, or you will not hold out."

To Pierre he said nothing, merely giving his arm a sympathetic squeeze below the shoulder. Pierre went with Anna Mikháylovna into the small drawing room.

"There is nothing so refreshing after a sleepless night as a cup of this delicious Russian tea," Lorrain was saying with an air of restrained animation as he stood sipping tea from a delicate Chinese handleless cup before a table on which tea and a cold supper were laid in the small circular room. Around the table all who were at Count Bezúkhov's house that night had gathered to fortify themselves. Pierre well remembered this small circular drawing room with its mirrors and little tables. During balls given at the house Pierre, who did not know how to dance, had liked sitting in this room to watch the ladies who, as they passed through in their ball dresses with diamonds and pearls on their bare shoulders, looked at themselves in the brilliantly lighted mirrors which repeated their reflections several times. Now this same room was dimly lighted by two candles. On one small table tea things and supper dishes stood in disorder, and in the middle of the night a motley throng of people sat there, not merrymaking, but somberly whispering, and betraying by every word and movement that they none of them forgot what was happening and what was about to happen in the bedroom. Pierre did not eat anything though he would very much have liked to. He looked inquiringly at his monitress and saw that she was again going on tiptoe to the reception room where they had left Prince Vasíli and the eldest princess. Pierre concluded that this also was essential, and after a short interval followed her. Anna Mikháylovna was standing beside the princess, and they were both speaking in excited whispers.

"Permit me, Princess, to know what is necessary and what is not necessary," said the younger of the two speakers, evidently in the same state of excitement as when she had slammed the door of her room.

"But, my dear princess," answered Anna Mikháylovna blandly but impressively, blocking the way to the bedroom and preventing the other from passing, "won't this be too much for poor Uncle at a moment when he needs repose? Worldly conversation at a moment when his soul is already prepared..."

Prince Vasíli was seated in an easy chair in his familiar attitude, with one leg crossed high above the other. His cheeks, which were so flabby that they looked heavier below, were twitching violently; but he wore the air of a man little concerned in what the two ladies were saying.

"Come, my dear Anna Mikháylovna, let Catiche do as she pleases. You know how fond the count is of her."

"I don't even know what is in this paper," said the younger of the two ladies, addressing Prince Vasíli and pointing to an inlaid portfolio she held in her hand. "All I know is that his real will is in his writing table, and this is a paper he has forgotten..."

She tried to pass Anna Mikháylovna, but the latter sprang so as to bar her path.

"I know, my dear, kind princess," said Anna Mikháylovna, seizing the portfolio so firmly that it was plain she would not let go easily. "Dear princess, I beg and implore you, have some pity on him! *Je vousen conjure...*"

The princess did not reply. Their efforts in the struggle for the portfolio were the only sounds audible, but it was evident that if the princess did speak, her words would not be flattering to Anna Mikháylovna. Though the latter held on tenaciously, her voice lost none of its honeyed firmness and softness.

"Pierre, my dear, come here. I think he will not be out of place in a family consultation; is it not so, Prince?"

"Why don't you speak, cousin?" suddenly shrieked the princess so loud that those in the drawing room heard her and were startled. "Why do you remain silent when heaven knows who permits herself to interfere, making a scene on the very threshold of a dying man's room? Intriguer!" she hissed viciously, and tugged with all her might at the portfolio.

But Anna Mikháylovna went forward a step or two to keep her hold on the portfolio, and changed her grip.

Prince Vasíli rose. "Oh!" said he with reproach and surprise, "this is absurd! Come, let go I tell you."

The princess let go.

"And you too!"

But Anna Mikháylovna did not obey him.

"Let go, I tell you! I will take the responsibility. I myself will go and ask him, I!... does that satisfy you?"

"But, Prince," said Anna Mikháylovna, "after such a solemn sacrament, allow him a moment's peace! Here, Pierre, tell them your opinion," said she, turning to the young man who, having come quite close, was gazing with astonishment at the angry face of the princess which had lost all dignity, and at the twitching cheeks of Prince Vasíli.

"Remember that you will answer for the consequences," said Prince Vasíli severely. "You don't know what you are doing."

"Vile woman!" shouted the princess, darting unexpectedly at Anna Mikháylovna and snatching the portfolio from her.

Prince Vasíli bent his head and spread out his hands.

At this moment that terrible door, which Pierre had watched so long and which had always opened so quietly, burst noisily open and banged against the wall, and the second of the three sisters rushed out wringing her hands.

"What are you doing!" she cried vehemently. "He is dying and you leave me alone with him!"

Her sister dropped the portfolio. Anna Mikháylovna, stooping, quickly caught up the object of contention and ran into the bedroom. The eldest princess and Prince Vasíli, recovering themselves, followed her. A few minutes later the eldest sister came out with a pale hard face, again biting her underlip. At sight of Pierre her expression showed an irrepressible hatred.

"Yes, now you may be glad!" said she; "this is what you have been waiting for." And bursting into tears she hid her face in her handkerchief and rushed from the room.

Prince Vasíli came next. He staggered to the sofa on which Pierre was sitting and dropped onto it, covering his face with his hand. Pierre noticed that he was pale and that his jaw quivered and shook as if in an ague.

"Ah, my friend!" said he, taking Pierre by the elbow; and there was in his voice a sincerity and weakness Pierre had never observed in it before. "How often we sin, how much we deceive, and all for what? I am near sixty, dear friend... I too... All will end in death, all! Death is awful..." and he burst into tears.

Anna Mikháylovna came out last. She approached Pierre with slow, quiet steps.

"Pierre!" she said.

Pierre gave her an inquiring look. She kissed the young man on his forehead, wetting him with her tears. Then after a pause she said:

"He is no more...."

Pierre looked at her over his spectacles.

"Come, I will go with you. Try to weep, nothing gives such relief as tears."

She led him into the dark drawing room and Pierre was glad no one could see his face. Anna Mikháylovna left him, and when she returned he was fast asleep with his head on his arm.

In the morning Anna Mikháylovna said to Pierre:

"Yes, my dear, this is a great loss for us all, not to speak of you. But God will support you: you are young, and are now, I hope, in command of an immense fortune. The will has not yet been opened. I know you well enough to be sure that this will not turn your head, but it imposes duties on you, and you must be a man."

Pierre was silent.

"Perhaps later on I may tell you, my dear boy, that if I had not been there, God only knows what would have happened! You know, Uncle promised me only the day before yesterday not to forget Borís. But he had no time. I hope, my dear friend, you will carry out your father's wish?"

Pierre understood nothing of all this and coloring shyly looked in silence at Princess Anna Mikháylovna. After her talk with Pierre, Anna Mikháylovna returned to the Rostóvs' and went to bed. On waking in the morning she told the Rostóvs and all her acquaintances the details of Count Bezúkhov's death. She said the count had died as she would herself wish to die, that his end was not only touching but edifying. As to the last meeting between father and son, it was so touching that she could not think of it without tears, and did not know which had behaved better during those awful moments—the father who so remembered everything and everybody at last and had spoken such pathetic words to the son, or Pierre, whom it had been pitiful to see, so stricken was he with grief, though he tried hard to hide it in order not to sadden his dying father. "It is painful, but it does one good. It uplifts the soul to see such men as the old count and his worthy son," said she. Of the behavior of the eldest princess and Prince Vasíli she spoke disapprovingly, but in whispers and as a great secret.

CHAPTER XXV

At Bald Hills, Prince Nicholas AndréevichBolkónski's estate, the arrival of young Prince Andrew and his wife was daily expected, but this expectation did not upset the regular routine of life in the old prince's household. General in Chief Prince Nicholas Andréevich (nicknamed in society, "the King of Prussia") ever since the Emperor Paul had exiled him to his country estate had lived there continuously with his daughter, Princess Mary, and her companion, Mademoiselle Bourienne. Though in the new reign he was free to return to the capitals, he still continued to live in the country, remarking that anyone who wanted to see him could come the hundred miles from Moscow to Bald Hills, while he himself needed no one and nothing. He used to say that there are only two sources of human vice—idleness and superstition, and only two virtues—activity and intelligence. He himself undertook his daughter's education, and to develop these two cardinal virtues in her gave her lessons in algebra and geometry till she was twenty, and arranged her life so that her whole time was occupied. He was himself always occupied: writing his memoirs, solving problems in higher mathematics, turning snuffboxes on a lathe, working in the garden, or superintending the building that was always going on at his estate. As regularity is a prime condition facilitating activity, regularity in his household was carried to the highest point of exactitude. He always came to table under precisely the same conditions, and not only at the same hour but at the same minute. With those about him, from his daughter to his serfs, the prince was sharp and invariably exacting, so that without being a hardhearted man he inspired such fear and respect as few hardhearted men would have aroused. Although he was in retirement and had now no influence in political affairs, every high official appointed to the province in which the prince's estate lay considered it his duty to visit him and waited in the lofty antechamber just as the architect, gardener, or Princess Mary did, till the prince appeared punctually to the appointed hour. Everyone sitting in this antechamber experienced the same feeling of respect and even fear when the enormously high study door opened and showed the figure of a rather small old man, with powdered wig, small withered hands, and bushy gray eyebrows which, when he frowned, sometimes hid the gleam of his shrewd, youthfully glittering eyes.

On the morning of the day that the young couple were to arrive, Princess Mary entered the antechamber as usual at the time appointed for the morning greeting, crossing herself with trepidation and repeating a silent prayer. Every morning she came in like that, and every morning prayed that the daily interview might pass off well.

An old powdered manservant who was sitting in the antechamber rose quietly and said in a whisper: "Please walk in."

Through the door came the regular hum of a lathe. The princess timidly opened the door which moved noiselessly and easily. She paused at the entrance. The prince was working at the lathe and after glancing round continued his work.

The enormous study was full of things evidently in constant use. The large table covered with books and plans, the tall glass-fronted bookcases with keys in the locks, the high desk for writing while standing up, on which lay an open exercise book, and the lathe with tools laid ready to hand and shavings scattered around—all indicated continuous, varied, and orderly activity. The motion of the small foot shod in a Tartar boot embroidered with silver, and the firm pressure of the lean sinewy hand, showed that the prince still possessed the tenacious endurance and vigor of hardy old age. After a few more turns of the lathe he removed his foot from the pedal, wiped his chisel, dropped it into a leather pouch attached to the lathe, and, approaching the table, summoned his daughter. He never gave his children a blessing, so he simply held out his bristly cheek (as yet unshaven) and, regarding her tenderly and attentively, said severely:

"Quite well? All right then, sit down." He took the exercise book containing lessons in geometry written by himself and drew up a chair with his foot.

"For tomorrow!" said he, quickly finding the page and making a scratch from one paragraph to another with his hard nail.

The princess bent over the exercise book on the table.

"Wait a bit, here's a letter for you," said the old man suddenly, taking a letter addressed in a woman's hand from a bag hanging above the table, onto which he threw it.

At the sight of the letter red patches showed themselves on the princess' face. She took it quickly and bent her head over it.

"From Héloïse?" asked the prince with a cold smile that showed his still sound, yellowish teeth.

"Yes, it's from Julie," replied the princess with a timid glance and a timid smile.

"I'll let two more letters pass, but the third I'll read," said the prince sternly; "I'm afraid you write much nonsense. I'll read the third!"

"Read this if you like, Father," said the princess, blushing still more and holding out the letter.

"The third, I said the third!" cried the prince abruptly, pushing the letter away, and leaning his elbows on the table he drew toward him the exercise book containing geometrical figures.

"Well, madam," he began, stooping over the book close to his daughter and placing an arm on the back of the chair on which she sat, so that she felt herself surrounded on all sides by the acrid scent of old age and tobacco, which she had known so long. "Now, madam, these triangles are equal; please note that the angle ABC..."

The princess looked in a scared way at her father's eyes glittering close to her; the red patches on her face came and went, and it was plain that she understood nothing and was so frightened that her fear would prevent her understanding any of her father's further explanations, however clear they might be. Whether it was the teacher's fault or the pupil's, this same thing happened every day: the princess' eyes grew dim, she could not see and could not hear anything, but was only conscious of her stern father's withered face close to her, of his breath and the smell of him, and could think only of how to get away quickly to her own room to make out the problem in peace. The old man was beside himself: moved the chair on which he was sitting noisily backward and forward, made efforts to control himself and not become vehement, but almost always did become vehement, scolded, and sometimes flung the exercise book away.

The princess gave a wrong answer.

"Well now, isn't she a fool!" shouted the prince, pushing the book aside and turning sharply away; but rising immediately, he paced up and down, lightly touched his daughter's hair and sat down again.

He drew up his chair, and continued to explain.

"This won't do, Princess; it won't do," said he, when Princess Mary, having taken and closed the exercise book with the next day's lesson, was about to leave: "Mathematics are most important, madam! I don't want to have you like our silly ladies. Get used to it and you'll like it," and he patted her cheek. "It will drive all the nonsense out of your head."

She turned to go, but he stopped her with a gesture and took an uncut book from the high desk.

"Here is some sort of *Key to the Mysteries* that your Héloïse has sent you. Religious! I don't interfere with anyone's belief... I have looked at it. Take it. Well, now go. Go."

He patted her on the shoulder and himself closed the door after her.

Princess Mary went back to her room with the sad, scared expression that rarely left her and which made her plain, sickly face yet plainer. She sat down at her writing table, on which stood miniature portraits and which was littered with books and papers. The princess was as untidy as her father was tidy. She put down the geometry book and eagerly broke the seal of her letter. It was from her most intimate friend from childhood; that same Julie Karágina who had been at the Rostóvs' name-day party.

Julie wrote in French:

Dear and precious Friend, How terrible and frightful a thing is separation! Though I tell myself that half my life and half my happiness are wrapped up in you, and that in spite of the distance separating us our hearts are united by indissoluble bonds, my heart rebels against fate and in spite of the pleasures and distractions around me I cannot overcome a certain secret sorrow that has been in my heart ever since we parted. Why are we not together as we were last summer, in your big study, on the blue sofa, the confidential sofa? Why cannot I now, as three months ago, draw fresh moral strength from your look, so gentle, calm, and penetrating, a look I loved so well and seem to see before me as I write?

Having read thus far, Princess Mary sighed and glanced into the mirror which stood on her right. It reflected a weak, ungraceful figure and thin face. Her eyes, always sad, now looked with particular hopelessness at her reflection in the glass. "She flatters me," thought the princess, turning away and continuing to read. But Julie did not flatter her friend, the princess' eyes—large, deep and luminous (it seemed as if at times there radiated from them shafts of warm light)—were so beautiful that very often in spite of the plainness of her face they gave her an attraction more powerful than that of beauty. But the princess never saw the beautiful expression of her own eyes—the look they had when she was not thinking of herself. As with everyone, her face assumed a forced unnatural expression as soon as she looked in a glass. She went on reading:

All Moscow talks of nothing but war. One of my two brothers is already abroad, the other is with the Guards, who are starting on their march to the frontier. Our dear Emperor has left Petersburg and it is thought intends to expose his precious person to the chances of war. God grant that the Corsican monster who is destroying the peace of Europe may be overthrown by the angel whom it has pleased the Almighty, in His goodness, to give us as sovereign! To say nothing of my brothers, this war has deprived me of one of the associations nearest my heart. I mean young Nicholas Rostóv, who with his enthusiasm could not bear to remain inactive and has left the university to join the army. I will confess to you, dear Mary, that in spite of his extreme youth his departure for the army was a great grief to me. This young man, of whom I spoke to you last summer, is so noble-minded and full of that real youthfulness which one seldom finds nowadays among our old men of twenty and, particularly, he is so frank and has so much heart. He is so pure and poetic that my relations with him, transient as they were, have been one of the sweetest comforts to my poor heart, which has already suffered so much. Someday I will tell you about our parting and all that was said then. That is still too fresh. Ah, dear friend, you are happy not to know these poignant joys and sorrows. You are fortunate, for the latter are generally the stronger! I know very well that Count Nicholas is too young ever to be more to me than a friend, but this sweet friendship, this poetic and pure intimacy, were what my heart needed. But enough of this! The chief news, about which all Moscow gossips, is the death of old Count Bezúkhov, and his inheritance. Fancy! The three princesses have received very little, Prince Vasíli nothing, and it is Monsieur Pierre who has inherited all the property and has besides been recognized as legitimate; so that he is now Count Bezúkhov and possessor of the finest fortune in Russia. It is rumored that Prince Vasíli played a very despicable part in this affair and that he returned to Petersburg quite crestfallen.

I confess I understand very little about all these matters of wills and inheritance; but I do know that since this young man, whom we all used to know as plain Monsieur Pierre, has become Count Bezúkhov and the owner of one of the largest fortunes in Russia, I am much amused to watch the change in the tone and manners of the mammas burdened by marriageable daughters, and of the young ladies themselves, toward him, though, between you and me, he always seemed to me a poor sort of fellow. As for the past two years people have amused themselves by finding husbands for me (most of whom I don't even know), the matchmaking chronicles of Moscow now speak of me as the future Countess Bezúkhova. But you will understand that I have no desire for the post. *À propos* of marriages: do you know that a while ago that *universal auntie* Anna Mikháylovna told me, under the seal of strict secrecy, of a plan of marriage for you. It is neither more nor less than with Prince Vasíli's son Anatole, whom they wish to reform by marrying him to someone rich and *distinguée*, and it is on you that his relations' choice has fallen. I don't know what you will think of it, but I consider it my duty to let you know of it. He is said to be very handsome and a terrible scapegrace. That is all I have been able to find out about him.

But enough of gossip. I am at the end of my second sheet of paper, and Mamma has sent for me to go and dine at the Apráksins'. Read the mystical book I am sending you; it has an enormous success here. Though there are things in it difficult for the feeble human mind to grasp, it is an admirable book which calms and elevates the soul. Adieu! Give my respects to monsieur your father and my compliments to Mademoiselle Bourienne. I embrace you as I love you.

JULIE

P.S. Let me have news of your brother and his charming little wife.

The princess pondered awhile with a thoughtful smile and her luminous eyes lit up so that her face was entirely transformed. Then she suddenly rose and with her heavy tread went up to the table. She took a sheet of paper and her hand moved rapidly over it. This is the reply she wrote, also in French:

Dear and precious Friend, Your letter of the 13th has given me great delight. So you still love me, my romantic Julie? Separation, of which you say so much that is bad, does not seem to have had its usual effect on you. You complain of our separation. What then should I say, if I *dared* complain, I who am deprived of all who are dear to me? Ah, if we had not religion to console us life would be very sad. Why do you suppose that I should look severely on your affection for that young man? On such matters I am only severe with myself. I understand such feelings in others, and if never having felt them I cannot approve of them, neither do I condemn them. Only it seems to me that Christian love, love of one's neighbor, love of one's enemy, is worthier, sweeter, and better than the feelings which the beautiful eyes of a young man can inspire in a romantic and loving young girl like yourself.

The news of Count Bezúkhov's death reached us before your letter and my father was much affected by it. He says the count was the last representative but one of the great century, and that it is his own turn now, but that he will do all he can to let his turn come as late as possible. God preserve us from that terrible misfortune!

I cannot agree with you about Pierre, whom I knew as a child. He always seemed to me to have an excellent heart, and that is the quality I value most in people. As to his inheritance and the part played by Prince Vasíli, it is very sad for both. Ah, my dear friend, our divine Saviour's words, that it is easier for a camel to go through the eye of a needle than for a rich man to enter the Kingdom of God, are terribly true. I pity Prince Vasíli but am still more sorry for Pierre. So young, and burdened with such riches—to what temptations he will be exposed! If I were asked what I desire most on earth, it would be to be poorer than the poorest beggar. A thousand thanks, dear friend, for the volume you have sent me and which has such success in Moscow. Yet since you tell me that among some good things it contains others which our weak human understanding cannot grasp, it seems to me rather useless to spend time in reading what is unintelligible and can therefore bear no fruit. I never could understand the fondness some people have for confusing their minds by dwelling on mystical books that merely awaken their doubts and excite their imagination, giving them a bent for exaggeration quite contrary to Christian simplicity. Let us rather read the Epistles and Gospels. Let us not seek to penetrate what mysteries they contain; for how can we, miserable sinners that we are, know the terrible and holy secrets of Providence while we remain in this flesh which forms an impenetrable veil between us and the Eternal? Let us rather confine ourselves to studying those sublime rules which our divine Saviour has left for our guidance here below. Let us try to conform to them and follow them, and let us be persuaded that the less we let our feeble human minds roam, the better we shall please God, who rejects all knowledge that does not come from Him; and the less we seek to fathom what He has been pleased to conceal from us, the sooner will He vouchsafe its revelation to us through His divine Spirit.

My father has not spoken to me of a suitor, but has only told me that he has received a letter and is expecting a visit from Prince Vasíli. In regard to this project of marriage for me, I will tell you, dear sweet friend, that I look on marriage as a divine institution to which we must conform. However painful it may be to me, should the Almighty lay the duties of wife and mother upon me I shall try to perform them as faithfully as I can, without disquieting myself by examining my feelings toward him whom He may give me for husband.

I have had a letter from my brother, who announces his speedy arrival at Bald Hills with his wife. This pleasure will be but a brief one, however, for he will leave us again to take part in this unhappy war into which we have been drawn, God knows how or why. Not only where you are—at the heart of affairs and of the world—is the talk all of war, even here amid fieldwork and the calm of nature—which townsfolk consider characteristic of the country—rumors of war are heard and painfully felt. My father talks of nothing but marches and countermarches, things of which I understand nothing; and the day before yesterday during my daily walk through the village I witnessed a heartrending scene.... It was a convoy of conscripts enrolled from our people and starting to join the army. You should have seen the state of the mothers, wives, and children of the men who were going and should have heard the sobs. It seems as though mankind has forgotten the laws of its divine Saviour, Who preached love and forgiveness of injuries—and that men attribute the greatest merit to skill in killing one another.

Adieu, dear and kind friend; may our divine Saviour and His most Holy Mother keep you in their holy and all-powerful care!

MARY

"Ah, you are sending off a letter, Princess? I have already dispatched mine. I have written to my poor mother," said the smiling Mademoiselle Bourienne rapidly, in her pleasant mellow tones and with guttural *r*'s. She brought into Princess Mary's strenuous, mournful, and gloomy world a quite different atmosphere, careless, lighthearted, and self-satisfied.

"Princess, I must warn you," she added, lowering her voice and evidently listening to herself with pleasure, and speaking with exaggerated *grasseyement*, "the prince has been scolding Michael Ivánovich. He is in a very bad humor, very morose. Be prepared."

"Ah, dear friend," replied Princess Mary, "I have asked you never to warn me of the humor my father is in. I do not allow myself to judge him and would not have others do so."

The princess glanced at her watch and, seeing that she was five minutes late in starting her practice on the clavichord, went into the sitting room with a look of alarm. Between twelve and two o'clock, as the day was mapped out, the prince rested and the princess played the clavichord.

CHAPTER XXVI

The gray-haired valet was sitting drowsily listening to the snoring of the prince, who was in his large study. From the far side of the house through the closed doors came the sound of difficult passages—twenty times repeated—of a sonata by Dussek.

Just then a closed carriage and another with a hood drove up to the porch. Prince Andrew got out of the carriage, helped his little wife to alight, and let her pass into the house before him. Old Tíkhon, wearing a wig, put his head out of the door of the antechamber, reported in a whisper that the prince was sleeping, and hastily closed the door. Tíkhon knew that neither the son's arrival nor any other unusual event must be allowed to disturb the appointed order of the day. Prince Andrew apparently knew this as well as Tíkhon; he looked at his watch as if to ascertain whether his father's habits had changed since he was at home last, and, having assured himself that they had not, he turned to his wife.

"He will get up in twenty minutes. Let us go across to Mary's room," he said.

The little princess had grown stouter during this time, but her eyes and her short, downy, smiling lip lifted when she began to speak just as merrily and prettily as ever.

"Why, this is a palace!" she said to her husband, looking around with the expression with which people compliment their host at a ball. "Let's come, quick, quick!" And with a glance round, she smiled at Tíkhon, at her husband, and at the footman who accompanied them.

"Is that Mary practicing? Let's go quietly and take her by surprise."

Prince Andrew followed her with a courteous but sad expression.

"You've grown older, Tíkhon," he said in passing to the old man, who kissed his hand.

Before they reached the room from which the sounds of the clavichord came, the pretty, fair-haired Frenchwoman, Mademoiselle Bourienne, rushed out apparently beside herself with delight.

"Ah! what joy for the princess!" exclaimed she: "At last! I must let her know."

"No, no, please not... You are Mademoiselle Bourienne," said the little princess, kissing her. "I know you already through my sister-in-law's friendship for you. She was not expecting us?"

They went up to the door of the sitting room from which came the sound of the oft-repeated passage of the sonata. Prince Andrew stopped and made a grimace, as if expecting something unpleasant.

The little princess entered the room. The passage broke off in the middle, a cry was heard, then Princess Mary's heavy tread and the sound of kissing. When Prince Andrew went in the two princesses, who had only met once before for a short time at his wedding, were in each other's arms warmly pressing their lips to whatever place they happened to touch. Mademoiselle Bourienne stood near them pressing her hand to her heart, with a beatific smile and obviously equally ready to cry or to laugh. Prince Andrew shrugged his shoulders and frowned, as lovers of music do when they hear a false note. The two women let go of one another, and then, as if afraid of being too late, seized each other's hands, kissing them and pulling them away, and again began kissing each other on the face, and then to Prince Andrew's surprise both began to cry and kissed again. Mademoiselle Bourienne also began to cry. Prince Andrew evidently felt ill at ease, but to the two women it seemed quite natural that they should cry, and apparently it never entered their heads that it could have been otherwise at this meeting.

"Ah! my dear!... Ah! Mary!..." they suddenly exclaimed, and then laughed. "I dreamed last night..."—"You were not expecting us?..." "Ah! Mary, you have got thinner?..." "And you have grown stouter!..."

"I knew the princess at once," put in Mademoiselle Bourienne.

"And I had no idea!..." exclaimed Princess Mary. "Ah, Andrew, I did not see you."

Prince Andrew and his sister, hand in hand, kissed one another, and he told her she was still the same crybaby as ever. Princess Mary had turned toward her brother, and through her tears the loving, warm, gentle look of her large luminous eyes, very beautiful at that moment, rested on Prince Andrew's face.

The little princess talked incessantly, her short, downy upper lip continually and rapidly touching her rosy nether lip when necessary and drawing up again next moment when her face broke into a smile of glittering teeth and sparkling eyes. She told of an accident they had had on the Spásski Hill which might have been serious for her in her condition, and immediately after that informed them that she had left all her clothes in Petersburg and that heaven knew what she would have to dress in here; and that Andrew had quite changed, and that Kitty Odýntsova had married an old man, and that there was a suitor for Mary, a real one, but that they would talk of that later. Princess Mary was still looking silently at her brother and her beautiful eyes were full of love and sadness. It was plain that she was following a train of thought independent of her sister-in-law's words. In the midst of a description of the last Petersburg fete she addressed her brother:

"So you are really going to the war, Andrew?" she said sighing.

Lise sighed too.

"Yes, and even tomorrow," replied her brother.

"He is leaving me here, God knows why, when he might have had promotion..."

Princess Mary did not listen to the end, but continuing her train of thought turned to her sister-in-law with a tender glance at her figure.

"Is it certain?" she said.

The face of the little princess changed. She sighed and said: "Yes, quite certain. Ah! it is very dreadful..."

Her lip descended. She brought her face close to her sister-in-law's and unexpectedly again began to cry.

"She needs rest," said Prince Andrew with a frown. "Don't you, Lise? Take her to your room and I'll go to Father. How is he? Just the same?"

"Yes, just the same. Though I don't know what your opinion will be," answered the princess joyfully.

"And are the hours the same? And the walks in the avenues? And the lathe?" asked Prince Andrew with a scarcely perceptible smile which showed that, in spite of all his love and respect for his father, he was aware of his weaknesses.

"The hours are the same, and the lathe, and also the mathematics and my geometry lessons," said Princess Mary gleefully, as if her lessons in geometry were among the greatest delights of her life.

When the twenty minutes had elapsed and the time had come for the old prince to get up, Tíkhon came to call the young prince to his father. The old man made a departure from his usual routine in honor of his son's arrival: he gave orders to admit him to his apartments while he dressed for dinner. The old prince always dressed in old-fashioned style, wearing an antique coat and powdered hair; and when Prince Andrew entered his father's dressing room (not with the contemptuous look and manner he wore in drawing rooms, but with the animated face with which he talked to Pierre), the old man was sitting on a large leather-covered chair, wrapped in a powdering mantle, entrusting his head to Tíkhon.

"Ah! here's the warrior! Wants to vanquish Buonaparte?" said the old man, shaking his powdered head as much as the tail, which Tíkhon was holding fast to plait, would allow.

"You at least must tackle him properly, or else if he goes on like this he'll soon have us, too, for his subjects! How are you?" And he held out his cheek.

The old man was in a good temper after his nap before dinner. (He used to say that a nap "after dinner was silver—before dinner, golden.") He cast happy, sidelong glances at his son from under his thick, bushy eyebrows. Prince Andrew went up and kissed his father on the spot indicated to him. He made no reply on his father's favorite topic—making fun of the military men of the day, and more particularly of Bonaparte.

"Yes, Father, I have come to you and brought my wife who is pregnant," said Prince Andrew, following every movement of his father's face with an eager and respectful look. "How is your health?"

"Only fools and rakes fall ill, my boy. You know me: I am busy from morning till night and abstemious, so of course I am well."

"Thank God," said his son smiling.

"God has nothing to do with it! Well, go on," he continued, returning to his hobby; "tell me how the Germans have taught you to fight Bonaparte by this new science you call 'strategy.'"

Prince Andrew smiled.

"Give me time to collect my wits, Father," said he, with a smile that showed that his father's foibles did not prevent his son from loving and honoring him. "Why, I have not yet had time to settle down!"

"Nonsense, nonsense!" cried the old man, shaking his pigtail to see whether it was firmly plaited, and grasping his by the hand. "The house for your wife is ready. Princess Mary will take her there and show her over, and they'll talk nineteen to the dozen. That's their woman's way! I am glad to have her. Sit down and talk. About Mikhelson's army I understand—Tolstóy's too... a simultaneous expedition.... But what's the southern army to do? Prussia is neutral... I know that. What about Austria?" said he, rising from his chair and pacing up and down the room followed by Tíkhon, who ran after him, handing him different articles of clothing. "What of Sweden? How will they cross Pomerania?"

Prince Andrew, seeing that his father insisted, began—at first reluctantly, but gradually with more and more animation, and from habit changing unconsciously from Russian to French as he went on—to explain the plan of operation for the coming campaign. He explained how an army, ninety thousand strong, was to threaten Prussia so as to bring her out of her neutrality and draw her into the war; how part of that army was to join some Swedish forces at Stralsund; how two hundred and twenty thousand Austrians, with a hundred thousand Russians, were to operate in Italy and on the Rhine; how fifty thousand Russians and as many English were to land at Naples, and how a total force of five hundred thousand men was to attack the French from different sides. The old prince did not evince the least interest during this explanation, but as if he were not listening to it continued to dress while walking about, and three times unexpectedly interrupted. Once he stopped it by shouting: "The white one, the white one!"

This meant that Tíkhon was not handing him the waistcoat he wanted. Another time he interrupted, saying:

"And will she soon be confined?" and shaking his head reproachfully said: "That's bad! Go on, go on."

The third interruption came when Prince Andrew was finishing his description. The old man began to sing, in the cracked voice of old age: *"Malbrooks'enva-t-en guerre. Dieu saitquandreviendra."* *

* "Marlborough is going to the wars; God knows when he'll return."

His son only smiled.

"I don't say it's a plan I approve of," said the son; "I am only telling you what it is. Napoleon has also formed his plan by now, not worse than this one."

"Well, you've told me nothing new," and the old man repeated, meditatively and rapidly:

"Dieu saitquandreviendra. Go to the dining room."

CHAPTER XXVII

At the appointed hour the prince, powdered and shaven, entered the dining room where his daughter-in-law, Princess Mary, and Mademoiselle Bourienne were already awaiting him together with his architect, who by a strange caprice of his employer's was admitted to table though the position of that insignificant individual was such as could certainly not have caused him to expect that honor. The prince, who generally kept very strictly to social distinctions and rarely admitted even important government officials to his table, had unexpectedly selected Michael Ivánovich (who always went into a corner to blow his nose on his checked handkerchief) to illustrate the theory that all men are equals, and had more than once impressed on his daughter that Michael Ivánovich was "not a whit worse than you or I." At dinner the prince usually spoke to the taciturn Michael Ivánovich more often than to anyone else.

In the dining room, which like all the rooms in the house was exceedingly lofty, the members of the household and the footmen—one behind each chair—stood waiting for the prince to enter. The head butler, napkin on arm, was scanning the setting of the table, making signs to the footmen, and anxiously glancing from the clock to the door by which the prince was to enter. Prince Andrew was looking at a large gilt frame, new to him, containing the genealogical tree of the Princes Bolkónski, opposite which hung another such frame with a badly painted portrait (evidently by the hand of the artist belonging to the estate) of a ruling prince, in a crown—an alleged descendant of Rúrik and ancestor of the Bolkónskis. Prince Andrew, looking again at that genealogical tree, shook his head, laughing as a man laughs who looks at a portrait so characteristic of the original as to be amusing.

"How thoroughly like him that is!" he said to Princess Mary, who had come up to him.

Princess Mary looked at her brother in surprise. She did not understand what he was laughing at. Everything her father did inspired her with reverence and was beyond question.

"Everyone has his Achilles' heel," continued Prince Andrew. "Fancy, with *his* powerful mind, indulging in such nonsense!"

Princess Mary could not understand the boldness of her brother's criticism and was about to reply, when the expected footsteps were heard coming from the study. The prince walked in quickly and jauntily as was his wont, as if intentionally contrasting the briskness of his manners with the strict formality of his house. At that moment the great clock struck two and another with a shrill tone joined in from the drawing room. The prince stood still; his lively glittering eyes from under their thick, bushy eyebrows sternly scanned all present and rested on the little princess. She felt, as courtiers do when the Tsar enters, the sensation of fear and respect which the old man inspired in all around him. He stroked her hair and then patted her awkwardly on the back of her neck.

"I'm glad, glad, to see you," he said, looking attentively into her eyes, and then quickly went to his place and sat down. "Sit down, sit down! Sit down, Michael Ivánovich!"

He indicated a place beside him to his daughter-in-law. A footman moved the chair for her.

"Ho, ho!" said the old man, casting his eyes on her rounded figure. "You've been in a hurry. That's bad!"

He laughed in his usual dry, cold, unpleasant way, with his lips only and not with his eyes.

"You must walk, walk as much as possible, as much as possible," he said.

The little princess did not, or did not wish to, hear his words. She was silent and seemed confused. The prince asked her about her father, and she began to smile and talk. He asked about mutual acquaintances, and she became still more animated and chattered away giving him greetings from various people and retelling the town gossip.

"Countess Apráksina, poor thing, has lost her husband and she has cried her eyes out," she said, growing more and more lively.

As she became animated the prince looked at her more and more sternly, and suddenly, as if he had studied her sufficiently and had formed a definite idea of her, he turned away and addressed Michael Ivánovich.

"Well, Michael Ivánovich, our Bonaparte will be having a bad time of it. Prince Andrew" (he always spoke thus of his son) "has been telling me what forces are being collected against him! While you and I never thought much of him."

Michael Ivánovich did not at all know when "you and I" had said such things about Bonaparte, but understanding that he was wanted as a peg on which to hang the prince's favorite topic, he looked inquiringly at the young prince, wondering what would follow.

"He is a great tactician!" said the prince to his son, pointing to the architect.

And the conversation again turned on the war, on Bonaparte, and the generals and statesmen of the day. The old prince seemed convinced not only that all the men of the day were mere babies who did not know the A B C of war or of politics, and that Bonaparte was an insignificant little Frenchy, successful only because there were no longer any Potëmkins or Suvórovs left to oppose him; but he was also convinced that there were no political difficulties in Europe and no real war, but only a sort of puppet show at which the men of the day were playing, pretending to do something real. Prince Andrew gaily bore with his father's ridicule of the new men, and drew him on and listened to him with evident pleasure.

"The past always seems good," said he, "but did not Suvórov himself fall into a trap Moreau set him, and from which he did not know how to escape?"

"Who told you that? Who?" cried the prince. "Suvórov!" And he jerked away his plate, which Tíkhon briskly caught. "Suvórov!... Consider, Prince Andrew. Two... Frederick and Suvórov; Moreau!... Moreau would have been a prisoner if Suvórov had had a free hand; but he had the *Hofs-kriegs-wurst-schnapps-Rath* on his hands. It would have puzzled the devil himself! When you get there you'll find out what those *Hofs-kriegs-wurst-Raths* are! Suvórov couldn't manage them so what chance has Michael Kutúzov? No, my dear boy," he continued, "you and your generals won't get on against Buonaparte; you'll have to call in the French, so that birds of a feather may fight together. The German, Pahlen, has been sent to New York in America, to fetch the Frenchman, Moreau," he said, alluding to the invitation made that year to Moreau to enter the Russian service.... "Wonderful!... Were the Potëmkins, Suvórovs, and Orlóvs Germans? No, lad, either you fellows have all lost your wits, or I have outlived mine. May God help you, but we'll see what will happen. Buonaparte has become a great commander among them! Hm!..."

"I don't at all say that all the plans are good," said Prince Andrew, "I am only surprised at your opinion of Bonaparte. You may laugh as much as you like, but all the same Bonaparte is a great general!"

"Michael Ivánovich!" cried the old prince to the architect who, busy with his roast meat, hoped he had been forgotten: "Didn't I tell you Buonaparte was a great tactician? Here, he says the same thing."

"To be sure, your excellency," replied the architect.

The prince again laughed his frigid laugh.

"Buonaparte was born with a silver spoon in his mouth. He has got splendid soldiers. Besides he began by attacking Germans. And only idlers have failed to beat the Germans. Since the world began everybody has beaten the Germans. They beat no one—except one another. He made his reputation fighting them."

And the prince began explaining all the blunders which, according to him, Bonaparte had made in his campaigns and even in politics. His son made no rejoinder, but it was evident that whatever arguments were presented he was as little able as his father to change his opinion. He listened, refraining from a reply, and involuntarily wondered how this old man, living alone in the country for so many years, could know and discuss so minutely and acutely all the recent European military and political events.

"You think I'm an old man and don't understand the present state of affairs?" concluded his father. "But it troubles me. I don't sleep at night. Come now, where has this great commander of yours shown his skill?" he concluded.

"That would take too long to tell," answered the son.

"Well, then go off to your Buonaparte! Mademoiselle Bourienne, here's another admirer of that powder-monkey emperor of yours," he exclaimed in excellent French.

"You know, Prince, I am not a Bonapartist!"

"Dieu saitquandreviendra." hummed the prince out of tune and, with a laugh still more so, he quitted the table.

The little princess during the whole discussion and the rest of the dinner sat silent, glancing with a frightened look now at her father-in-law and now at Princess Mary. When they left the table she took her sister-in-law's arm and drew her into another room.

"What a clever man your father is," said she; "perhaps that is why I am afraid of him."

"Oh, he is so kind!" answered Princess Mary.

CHAPTER XXVIII

Prince Andrew was to leave next evening. The old prince, not altering his routine, retired as usual after dinner. The little princess was in her sister-in-law's room. Prince Andrew in a traveling coat without epaulettes had been packing with his valet in the rooms assigned to him. After inspecting the carriage himself and seeing the trunks put in, he ordered the horses to be harnessed. Only those things he always kept with him remained in his room; a small box, a large canteen fitted with silver plate, two Turkish pistols and a saber—a present from his father who had brought it from the siege of Ochákov. All these traveling effects of Prince Andrew's were in very good order: new, clean, and in cloth covers carefully tied with tapes.

When starting on a journey or changing their mode of life, men capable of reflection are generally in a serious frame of mind. At such moments one reviews the past and plans for the future. Prince Andrew's face looked very thoughtful and tender. With his hands behind him he paced briskly from corner to corner of the room, looking straight before him and thoughtfully shaking his head. Did he fear going to the war, or was he sad at leaving his wife?—perhaps both, but evidently he did not wish to be seen in that mood, for hearing footsteps in the passage he hurriedly unclasped his hands, stopped at a table as if tying the cover of the small box, and assumed his usual tranquil and impenetrable expression. It was the heavy tread of Princess Mary that he heard.

"I hear you have given orders to harness," she cried, panting (she had apparently been running), "and I did so wish to have another talk with you alone! God knows how long we may again be parted. You are not angry with me for coming? You have changed so, Andrúsha," she added, as if to explain such a question.

She smiled as she uttered his pet name, "Andrúsha." It was obviously strange to her to think that this stern handsome man should be Andrúsha—the slender mischievous boy who had been her playfellow in childhood.

"And where is Lise?" he asked, answering her question only by a smile.

"She was so tired that she has fallen asleep on the sofa in my room. Oh, Andrew! What a treasure of a wife you have," said she, sitting down on the sofa, facing her brother. "She is quite a child: such a dear, merry child. I have grown so fond of her."

Prince Andrew was silent, but the princess noticed the ironical and contemptuous look that showed itself on his face.

"One must be indulgent to little weaknesses; who is free from them, Andrew? Don't forget that she has grown up and been educated in society, and so her position now is not a rosy one. We should enter into everyone's situation. *Tout comprendre, c'est tout pardonner.* * Think what it must be for her, poor thing, after what she has been used to, to be parted from her husband and be left alone in the country, in her condition! It's very hard."

* To understand all is to forgive all.

Prince Andrew smiled as he looked at his sister, as we smile at those we think we thoroughly understand.

"You live in the country and don't think the life terrible," he replied.

"I... that's different. Why speak of me? I don't want any other life, and can't, for I know no other. But think, Andrew: for a young society woman to be buried in the country during the best years of her life, all alone—for Papa is always busy, and I... well, you know what poor resources I have for entertaining a woman used to the best society. There is only Mademoiselle Bourienne...."

"I don't like your Mademoiselle Bourienne at all," said Prince Andrew.

"No? She is very nice and kind and, above all, she's much to be pitied. She has no one, no one. To tell the truth, I don't need her, and she's even in my way. You know I always was a savage, and now am even more so. I like being alone.... Father likes her very much. She and Michael Ivánovich are the two people to whom he is always gentle and kind, because he has been a benefactor to them both. As Sterne says: 'We don't love people so much for the good they have done us, as for the good we have done them.' Father took her when she was homeless after losing her own father. She is very good-natured, and my father likes her way of reading. She reads to him in the evenings and reads splendidly."

"To be quite frank, Mary, I expect Father's character sometimes makes things trying for you, doesn't it?" Prince Andrew asked suddenly.

Princess Mary was first surprised and then aghast at this question.

"For me? For me?... Trying for me!..." said she.

"He always was rather harsh; and now I should think he's getting very trying," said Prince Andrew, apparently speaking lightly of their father in order to puzzle or test his sister.

"You are good in every way, Andrew, but you have a kind of intellectual pride," said the princess, following the train of her own thoughts rather than the trend of the conversation—"and that's a great sin. How can one judge Father? But even if one might, what feeling except veneration could such a man as my father evoke? And I am so contented and happy with him. I only wish you were all as happy as I am."

Her brother shook his head incredulously.

"The only thing that is hard for me... I will tell you the truth, Andrew... is Father's way of treating religious subjects. I don't understand how a man of his immense intellect can fail to see what is as clear as day, and can go so far astray. That is the only thing that makes me unhappy. But even in this I can see lately a shade of improvement. His satire has been less bitter of late, and there was a monk he received and had a long talk with."

"Ah! my dear, I am afraid you and your monk are wasting your powder," said Prince Andrew banteringly yet tenderly.

"Ah! *monami*, I only pray, and hope that God will hear me. Andrew..." she said timidly after a moment's silence, "I have a great favor to ask of you."

"What is it, dear?"

"No—promise that you will not refuse! It will give you no trouble and is nothing unworthy of you, but it will comfort me. Promise, Andrúsha!..." said she, putting her hand in her reticule but not yet taking out what she was holding inside it, as if what she held were the subject of her request and must not be shown before the request was granted.

She looked timidly at her brother.

"Even if it were a great deal of trouble..." answered Prince Andrew, as if guessing what it was about.

"Think what you please! I know you are just like Father. Think as you please, but do this for my sake! Please do! Father's father, our grandfather, wore it in all his wars." (She still did not take out what she was holding in her reticule.) "So you promise?"

"Of course. What is it?"

"Andrew, I bless you with this icon and you must promise me you will never take it off. Do you promise?"

"If it does not weigh a hundredweight and won't break my neck... To please you..." said Prince Andrew. But immediately, noticing the pained expression his joke had brought to his sister's face, he repented and added: "I am glad; really, dear, I am very glad."

"Against your will He will save and have mercy on you and bring you to Himself, for in Him alone is truth and peace," said she in a voice trembling with emotion, solemnly holding up in both hands before her brother a small, oval, antique, dark-faced icon of the Saviour in a gold setting, on a finely wrought silver chain.

She crossed herself, kissed the icon, and handed it to Andrew.

"Please, Andrew, for my sake!..."

Rays of gentle light shone from her large, timid eyes. Those eyes lit up the whole of her thin, sickly face and made it beautiful. Her brother would have taken the icon, but she stopped him. Andrew understood, crossed himself and kissed the icon. There was a look of tenderness, for he was touched, but also a gleam of irony on his face.

"Thank you, my dear." She kissed him on the forehead and sat down again on the sofa. They were silent for a while.

"As I was saying to you, Andrew, be kind and generous as you always used to be. Don't judge Lise harshly," she began. "She is so sweet, so good-natured, and her position now is a very hard one."

"I do not think I have complained of my wife to you, Másha, or blamed her. Why do you say all this to me?"

Red patches appeared on Princess Mary's face and she was silent as if she felt guilty.

"I have said nothing to you, but you have already been talked to. And I am sorry for that," he went on.

The patches grew deeper on her forehead, neck, and cheeks. She tried to say something but could not. Her brother had guessed right: the little princess had been crying after dinner and had spoken of her forebodings about her confinement, and how she dreaded it, and had complained of her fate, her father-in-law, and her husband. After crying she had fallen asleep. Prince Andrew felt sorry for his sister.

"Know this, Másha: I can't reproach, have not reproached, and never shall reproach *my wife* with anything, and I cannot reproach myself with anything in regard to her; and that always will be so in whatever circumstances I may be placed. But if you want to know the truth... if you want to know whether I am happy? No! Is she happy? No! But why this is so I don't know..."

As he said this he rose, went to his sister, and, stooping, kissed her forehead. His fine eyes lit up with a thoughtful, kindly, and unaccustomed brightness, but he was looking not at his sister but over her head toward the darkness of the open doorway.

"Let us go to her, I must say good-by. Or—go and wake and I'll come in a moment. Petrúshka!" he called to his valet: "Come here, take these away. Put this on the seat and this to the right."

Princess Mary rose and moved to the door, then stopped and said: "Andrew, if you had faith you would have turned to God and asked Him to give you the love you do not feel, and your prayer would have been answered."

"Well, maybe!" said Prince Andrew. "Go, Másha; I'll come immediately."

On the way to his sister's room, in the passage which connected one wing with the other, Prince Andrew met Mademoiselle Bourienne smiling sweetly. It was the third time that day that, with an ecstatic and artless smile, she had met him in secluded passages.

"Oh! I thought you were in your room," she said, for some reason blushing and dropping her eyes.

Prince Andrew looked sternly at her and an expression of anger suddenly came over his face. He said nothing to her but looked at her forehead and hair, without looking at her eyes, with such contempt that the Frenchwoman blushed and went away without a word. When he reached his sister's room his wife was already awake and her merry voice, hurrying one word after another, came through the open door. She was speaking as usual in French, and as if after long self-restraint she wished to make up for lost time.

"No, but imagine the old Countess Zúbova, with false curls and her mouth full of false teeth, as if she were trying to cheat old age.... Ha, ha, ha! Mary!"

This very sentence about Countess Zúbova and this same laugh Prince Andrew had already heard from his wife in the presence of others some five times. He entered the room softly. The little princess, plump and rosy, was sitting in an easy chair with her work in her hands, talking incessantly, repeating Petersburg reminiscences and even phrases. Prince Andrew came up, stroked her hair, and asked if she felt rested after their journey. She answered him and continued her chatter.

The coach with six horses was waiting at the porch. It was an autumn night, so dark that the coachman could not see the carriage pole. Servants with lanterns were bustling about in the porch. The immense house was brilliant with lights shining through its lofty windows. The domestic serfs were crowding in the hall, waiting to bid good-by to the young prince. The members of the household were all gathered in the reception hall: Michael Ivánovich, Mademoiselle Bourienne, Princess Mary, and the little princess. Prince Andrew had been called to his father's study as the latter wished to say good-by to him alone. All were waiting for them to come out.

When Prince Andrew entered the study the old man in his old-age spectacles and white dressing gown, in which he received no one but his son, sat at the table writing. He glanced round.

"Going?" And he went on writing.

"I've come to say good-by."

"Kiss me here," and he touched his cheek: "Thanks, thanks!"

"What do you thank me for?"

"For not dilly-dallying and not hanging to a woman's apron strings. The Service before everything. Thanks, thanks!" And he went on writing, so that his quill spluttered and squeaked. "If you have anything to say, say it. These two things can be done together," he added.

"About my wife... I am ashamed as it is to leave her on your hands...."

"Why talk nonsense? Say what you want."

"When her confinement is due, send to Moscow for an *accoucheur*.... Let him be here...."

The old prince stopped writing and, as if not understanding, fixed his stern eyes on his son.

"I know that no one can help if nature does not do her work," said Prince Andrew, evidently confused. "I know that out of a million cases only one goes wrong, but it is her fancy and mine. They have been telling her things. She has had a dream and is frightened."

"Hm... Hm..." muttered the old prince to himself, finishing what he was writing. "I'll do it."

He signed with a flourish and suddenly turning to his son began to laugh.

"It's a bad business, eh?"

"What is bad, Father?"

"The wife!" said the old prince, briefly and significantly.

"I don't understand!" said Prince Andrew.

"No, it can't be helped, lad," said the prince. "They're all like that; one can't unmarry. Don't be afraid; I won't tell anyone, but you know it yourself."

He seized his son by the hand with small bony fingers, shook it, looked straight into his son's face with keen eyes which seemed to see through him, and again laughed his frigid laugh.

The son sighed, thus admitting that his father had understood him. The old man continued to fold and seal his letter, snatching up and throwing down the wax, the seal, and the paper, with his accustomed rapidity.

"What's to be done? She's pretty! I will do everything. Make your mind easy," said he in abrupt sentences while sealing his letter.

Andrew did not speak; he was both pleased and displeased that his father understood him. The old man got up and gave the letter to his son.

"Listen!" said he; "don't worry about your wife: what can be done shall be. Now listen! Give this letter to Michael Ilariónovich. * I have written that he should make use of you in proper places and not keep you long as an adjutant: a bad position! Tell him I remember and like him. Write and tell me how he receives you. If he is all right—serve him. Nicholas Bolkónski's son need not serve under anyone if he is in disfavor. Now come here."

* Kutúzov.

He spoke so rapidly that he did not finish half his words, but his son was accustomed to understand him. He led him to the desk, raised the lid, drew out a drawer, and took out an exercise book filled with his bold, tall, close handwriting.

"I shall probably die before you. So remember, these are my memoirs; hand them to the Emperor after my death. Now here is a Lombard bond and a letter; it is a premium for the man who writes a history of Suvórov's wars. Send it to the Academy. Here are some jottings for you to read when I am gone. You will find them useful."

Andrew did not tell his father that he would no doubt live a long time yet. He felt that he must not say it.

"I will do it all, Father," he said.

"Well, now, good-by!" He gave his son his hand to kiss, and embraced him. "Remember this, Prince Andrew, if they kill you it will hurt me, your old father..." he paused unexpectedly, and then in a querulous voice suddenly shrieked: "but if I hear that you have not behaved like a son of Nicholas Bolkónski, I shall be ashamed!"

"You need not have said that to me, Father," said the son with a smile.

The old man was silent.

"I also wanted to ask you," continued Prince Andrew, "if I'm killed and if I have a son, do not let him be taken away from you—as I said yesterday... let him grow up with you.... Please."

"Not let the wife have him?" said the old man, and laughed.

They stood silent, facing one another. The old man's sharp eyes were fixed straight on his son's. Something twitched in the lower part of the old prince's face.

"We've said good-by. Go!" he suddenly shouted in a loud, angry voice, opening his door.

"What is it? What?" asked both princesses when they saw for a moment at the door Prince Andrew and the figure of the old man in a white dressing gown, spectacled and wigless, shouting in an angry voice.

Prince Andrew sighed and made no reply.

"Well!" he said, turning to his wife.

And this "Well!" sounded coldly ironic, as if he were saying: "Now go through your performance."

"Andrew, already!" said the little princess, turning pale and looking with dismay at her husband.

He embraced her. She screamed and fell unconscious on his shoulder.

He cautiously released the shoulder she leaned on, looked into her face, and carefully placed her in an easy chair.

"Adieu, Mary," said he gently to his sister, taking her by the hand and kissing her, and then he left the room with rapid steps.

The little princess lay in the armchair, Mademoiselle Bourienne chafing her temples. Princess Mary, supporting her sister-in-law, still looked with her beautiful eyes full of tears at the door through which Prince Andrew had gone and made the sign of the cross in his direction. From the study, like pistol shots, came the frequent sound of the old man angrily blowing his nose. Hardly had Prince Andrew gone when the study door opened quickly and the stern figure of the old man in the white dressing gown looked out.

"Gone? That's all right!" said he; and looking angrily at the unconscious little princess, he shook his head reprovingly and slammed the door.